ATTACKING EARTH AND SUN

ATTACKING EARTH AND SUN

MATHIEU BELEZI

*Translated from the French by
Lara Vergnaud*

OTHER PRESS
NEW YORK

Originally published in 2022 as *Attaquer la terre et le soleil*
by Le Tripode, Paris
Copyright © Le Tripode, 2022
Published by special arrangement with Éditions Le Tripode, France,
in conjunction with their duly appointed agents Books and More Agency

English translation copyright © Lara Vergnaud, 2025

Title-page art: Miloje / Shutterstock

Production editor: Yvonne E. Cárdenas
Text designer: Patrice Sheridan
This book was set in Chaparral Pro by
Alpha Design & Composition of Pittsfield, NH

1 3 5 7 9 10 8 6 4 2

Library of Congress Cataloging-in-Publication Data
Names: Belezi, Mathieu author | Vergnaud, Lara translator
Title: Attacking earth and sun / Mathieu Belezi ; translated from the
French by Lara Vergnaud.
Other titles: Attaquer la terre et le soleil. English
Description: New York : Other Press, 2025.
Identifiers: LCCN 2025007278 (print) | LCCN 2025007279 (ebook) |
ISBN 9781635425154 paperback | ISBN 9781635425161 ebook
Subjects: LCSH: Algeria—History—1830-1962—Fiction | Military
occupation—Fiction | LCGFT: Historical fiction | Novels
Classification: LCC PQ2662.E45125 A8813 2025 (print) |
LCC PQ2662.E45125 (ebook) | DDC 843/.914—dc23/eng/20250327
LC record available at https://lccn.loc.gov/2025007278
LC ebook record available at https://lccn.loc.gov/2025007279

Publisher's Note

This is a work of fiction. Names, characters, places, and incidents either are
the product of the author's imagination or are used fictitiously, and any
resemblance to actual persons, living or dead, events, or locales is entirely
coincidental.

A proliferating and overexcited civilization
has forever shattered the silence of the seas.
—Claude Lévi-Strauss

(HANDS OF TOIL)

I wept

    I couldn't help but weep when we arrived and saw the land that would need working

    holy Mary mother of God

    days and days of travel, along the Seine and the Saône, and then the Rhône on boats flat as the palm of your hand and drawn by horses that took their sweet time, believe you me, while at every lock the men raced to the inns to gorge themselves on food and wine as we poor women used the pause to wash the linens not to mention the children, days and days I'm telling you, until at last we could make out the sea, the sea and its dazzling light that beckoned like a beacon over the port of Marseille

    holy Mary mother of God

    then they crammed us and all the other wide-eyed migrants in a lazaretto, we were a good five hundred in there, five hundred with eyes peeled for the frigate *Labrador*, which wasn't in port and wouldn't be for a good week, five hundred quelling our impatience by strolling the city streets, five hundred seated on café terraces with the mistral at our backs or pressing our noses against novelty shop windows, until it was announced that the boat had arrived and we could board with our trunks and hodgepodge of furniture and household necessities

holy Mary mother of God

days and nights on that *Labrador* pitching like a cockleshell as we clutched our stomachs and emptied our guts before finally setting two feet on Algerian soil and listening to an army commander's fine words

"Rest assured, all you brave men and women gathered here, that the government of the Republic of France will watch over you like a father over his children. Day and night, on any occasion, we will be here to give you a hand. Whatever may come, never lose faith in your government, in your republic. Our eyes are wide open and our ears are pricked for any grievance you may voice. We will do everything in our power—everything, mind you!—to ensure that your hands of toil are fairly compensated. For you are the strength and intelligence France requires in these barbaric lands, you are its new bubbling blood. And nothing could be more precious"

fine, moving words duly followed by drumrolls and applause

"Vive la France! Vive la France!"

before being split into two groups and swiftly dispatched to two agricultural colonies that had been blindly mapped out by a few wretched bureaucrats, finally leaving Bône in the beds of army gun carriages, jolted along a road, what am I saying!, along a vague trail through fields and over rocky terrain before the nasty stares of filthy children and women wearing garish rags to hide their base instincts

"Don't look at them, Caro"

and I covered my children's eyes with my hands for fear that one of those harpies would cast a spell on them

"But, Mama, we want to see"

"You'll have plenty of time"

as skin-and-bone dogs bristled with what little hair remained on their backs and bared their rotten teeth and barked as they sniffed the soldiers' vinegary smell

and on it went all day long until our captain, perched on his horse, raised his arm and ordered

"Halt!"

it was evening, the silence of the sky casting a wide gloom, and behind our column the horizon was black with overlapping clouds jostling each other to get a better look at all these people who'd shown up with no warning, it was evening yet still light and in that dying light we saw rows of military tents, at least five or six, and we understood that beneath those folds of military canvas was where we would have to live but for how long? holy mother of God, how long?

and shelter from the sun and rain and savage wind roaring in rage, and not beneath the reassuring roofs of the houses promised us by the Republic of France, which would be built one day, not to worry, they said, one day soon, but what did that mean, one day soon? truly, what did it mean? didn't we realize that time is different on that cursed African continent, that days and weeks and months don't mean anything at all?

we were obliged to share a tent with a family from Aubervilliers every bit as bone-tired as ours was, Henri and I and our three children, and my sister Rosette and her husband, Louis, who never stopped coughing owing to his fragile lungs, the dust from the trip hadn't done him any good

fires had been lit around the camp and together we ate rations distributed by the soldiers, several of whom were to keep watch until dawn, pistols ready, the captain had promised

"What is there to fear, captain?"

"Everything, my friends, everything that prowls, creeps, and snarls, there are bands of pillagers and horned vipers, and of course the desert lions roaming these parts"

night came on faster than it does in France, it fell in one swoop and spread like a puddle of black ink, troubled and teeming with noises that frightened the children, above all Caroline, who cowered, trembling, against my stomach, while my two boys lying head to tail on a blanket kept sitting up to ask

"Mama, is Papa asleep?"

"I don't know"

but I knew perfectly well that Henri wasn't asleep, I imagined his eyes were as wide open as mine and that he was beginning to ask himself the same questions I had asked countless times before we left, questions he didn't listen to at the time, questions that he brushed away with a flick of his hand because to him they were women's questions and hell's bells! we won't get very far asking women's questions, he would shout, smoothing his mustache, which he kept thick but not always neat

the heaven on earth promised us by the Republic of France was far and we certainly wouldn't be reaching it anytime soon, crammed as we were into army tents in the middle of some godforsaken hole the brass dared call an "agricultural colony," no we wouldn't be reaching the heaven on everyone's lips anytime soon, maybe we never would, maybe we would never reach it because it didn't exist, it never had and never would exist, at least not for people like us

in spite of myself I felt a pang in my heart and my chest swell with the despair suddenly pouring over me, I clenched my fists to hold back the sobs rattling in my throat, though why bother? the gathering tears needed to come out, to fall, to run down my naked cheeks so I wept, face buried in the silence of a pillow that still smelled of the *Labrador*, stricken by a solitude that was too great, too heavy, too painful for me to bear, I wept every tear I had inside my body

holy Mary mother of God.

O

Come morning, the daylight trickling through the tent roof was gray, I rose early, awakened by the clanking of mess kits, and tiptoed over the slumbering bodies to step outside to see what this agricultural colony might look like, I rubbed my sleep-creased cheeks and took a good long look around, spinning right then left in search of something that might catch my eye and comfort me, might lift the dread making it hard for me to breathe, but I didn't find anything, and if I didn't find anything it's because there was nothing to see, nothing I tell you, not a thing

just scrub, rocks, and clouds so low they made you want to sink into the earth

and before me that ominous line of military tents that didn't belong in this desert any more than a hair does in a bowl of soup, as I made my way down the row I could hear grown-ups snoring and children moaning in their sleep, surely dreaming of a not-so-distant past when they used to play in the schoolyard, I shivered, caught in a gust of wind so cold that I wrapped myself even more tightly in the wool shawl covering my shoulders, I looked up at the menacing sky, it wasn't the same weather as yesterday, something had changed, it was chilly, the clouds darkening to black as I watched, soon they would burst overhead

at the back of the camp there were five or six soldiers up and about too, kindling fires for cooking, preparing marmites bubbling with a broth of meat, bones, and potatoes, there were pots of coffee already steaming and spreading a familiar smell through the air

"Care for some coffee, little lady?"

I went closer and a soldier handed me a tinplate cup into which he had splashed a bit of coffee, or rather a blackish liquid he called coffee that had the aroma but not the taste and which I drank all the same because it was warm, and that warmth traveled the length of my body, down to where my unshakable dread weighed heavy as a sheet of ice

I thanked him and continued on my way, leaving the soldiers to comment on my passing with words I preferred not to hear, one of them burst out laughing, which was when I turned around, rage flushing my cheeks, on the verge, I could tell, of exploding

"What is so funny, may I ask?"

"We're not making fun of you, m'dame, I swear"

said the soldier who had laughed

I shrugged and kept walking as it began to rain, cold, fat drops thundering against the tent canvas, a few struck me in the face and I hunched over to avoid the rest, arms tight around my waist, nails digging into the palms of my hands to rid myself of a rage that served no purpose.

○

It rained without interruption for a whole week, nasty torrents that seeped into everything and kept us from going outside, from venturing so much as a toe, we didn't dare move, trapped on our straw pallets for hours as we watched the rain leak through the soaked canvas that was all the shelter we had, dripping onto our things, our bags, blankets, and shoes, dampening our hair that would never again be completely dry, trickling down our necks, entering our pores to penetrate flesh and bone, taking possession of our limbs, of our arms and legs that we could no longer feel because the cold had frozen them stiff

and when the men went out, by which I mean Henri, Louis, and the old man from Aubervilliers, when they went out to dig a hole and light a fire, to try to warm up what our family and the Aubervilliers lot had brought from France (sausages, hams, and bacon that my father would send us every year from Auvergne), it took them forever to prepare a stew with the meat and the potatoes I had packed as a precaution, and then the woman from Aubervilliers wanted to add the turnips she had bought in Marseille, as a precaution too

and this went on for eight days, what am I saying? ten days, the endless rain battering our colony, which was by then a cluster of waterlogged tents at perennial risk of being blown away by angry gusts, and which required constant patching and plugging so they wouldn't collapse into the foul mud, not to mention the urine and shit, for our children paralyzed with fear had no choice but to squat in any and all corners of the tent to relieve themselves, and soon the smell was unbearable, unbreathable, in our tent same as the others where children were stuck day and night

once a day, accompanied by Rosette and Célestine, the woman from Aubervilliers who in a few days of communal living had become like another sister, the three of us holding hands and walking blindly through the sheets of rain, once a day and sometimes twice, I would urinate behind a bush, and as I squatted, eyes closed like I was praying beneath the hood of my cape, I would force myself to believe that it was all just a bad dream, and that to escape I simply needed to throw back the covers and the nightmare would end, the rain, the cold, the mud, the stench of our neglected bodies, all of it would suddenly stop, Don't worry, Séraphine, you're having a bad dream, you're dreaming, sweet girl, simply dreaming, come on wake up now and you'll see that you've never set foot, thank heaven, on the soil of this cursed colony, but then I would open my eyes and see straightaway that I wasn't dreaming, and the reality was so dreadful that tears would flood my face already dripping with rain, sometimes I would tumble backward into the mud, arms extended to catch hold of a branch, and I would have let myself die there wallowing in that mud if my sister and Célestine hadn't come to my rescue, but each time they rushed to help me, putting their arms under my shoulders to stand me back up

"Be strong, Séraphine, I'm begging you"

Rosette would cry out in her familiar sisterly voice, which always took a moment to penetrate the curtain of rain, she'd be forced to shake me and rub my frozen cheeks with her washerwoman hands

"Get ahold of yourself"

yes, I did need to get ahold of myself, to find the will to fight, if not for me at least for my children, who only wanted to live, to get through these hard times in the shelter of my maternal arms that were as necessary to them as a mother dog's belly to her three pups

so then I held tight to Rosette's waist and Célestine's arm, and the three of us would wade through the mire of that wretched land that with every step sought to make us stumble, to bring us down and maybe even suffocate us in its awful sludge, maybe even swallow us down to the depths of its hell, our bodies and belongings vanished, crushed, torn to shreds, digested, that's how certain I was that our place wasn't here, that it had never been and would never be here

holy Mary mother of God

and it was only once we were back in the tent that I caught my breath and collected myself

holy Mary mother of God

I wiped my rain-drenched face and, opening my eyes again, instinctively reached for my children, whom I embraced as tightly as my strength allowed

what else could I have done?

○

Three months it lasted, three months the rotten weather kept us holed up in our military tents in endless need of patching and mending and fortifying with ropes and stakes, so relentless was the onslaught of wind and rain from sunup to sundown

shut away like hogs in a sty, hands and faces black with grime, hair wild, caked in mud up to our bellies with no way to get clean, our insides cramped and twisted, under constant attack by the slop the soldiers served us and the foul odors given off by bodies abandoned to their own devices, a stench of piss, shit, sweat, and soggy skin macerating beneath layers of never-washed clothes

as if each of us poor naive settlers barely off the boat was already starting to rot and decompose

and the captain on his inspection rounds could tell us as often as he liked

"Hold fast, friends, spring is coming!"

but, shivering with fever and despair, we lost a little more of what remained of our dignity with each passing day

yet the captain was right, spring did come in the end, and with it army engineers sent by Algiers to come to our aid and build us our houses, or rather what we liked to call houses to cheer ourselves up but that were in truth wooden shacks to be shared with other families

so poorly were the planks sealed that the wind, dust, sun, and rain soon made themselves at home, leaving us little protection, the same way the gaps in the wood let the colony's peeping Toms rob us of our privacy, thankfully we ended up with the family from Aubervilliers, sharing a tent for an entire winter creates bonds, it does, and we could have had it worse than living in close quarters with Célestine, her elderly father, and her two boys

and before the sawdust had settled we were dragging our straw pallets onto a wood floor that smelled sweetly of sap, along with our rickety sideboard, the two chairs we had remaining after the others were stolen, and our woefully damp and moldy linens, and I couldn't say why but when I opened my eyes one April morning, properly rested after a good night's sleep, I felt reassured at last, joyful almost inside those wooden walls, it was a fine day, the sky clear from one side of the horizon to the other, and the rising sun had painted the roofs gold as if it too wanted the best for us

holy Mary mother of God who comes to our aid, praised be

the air was as transparent and pure as crystal, and in that unrivaled pureness the sounds of saws and hammers, birds' trilling, and men's heave-hos echoed like in a cathedral

Henri and Louis finished nailing the door that would at last offer us protection from everything, desert lions and yataghan-wielding barbarians alike, I went closer to touch the wood, which was thicker than the walls, as though I needed to reassure myself, and letting out a sigh of relief I asked them

"Would you like some coffee?"

"Of course"

they responded in chorus

I knew that there wasn't a single bean to grind from our meager supply of coffee from France, which we had exhausted over the winter, that all I could do was pour hot water over dregs of roasted barley, which I did, wedging the pot between the large hearthstones that served as our stove, then I kindled the fire with dry branches and as I waited for the water to boil watched geckos scamper away, a colony of ants marching back and forth in single file, and other insects that I couldn't have named, I'd never seen them before and yet I'm sure they had existed since long before I was born

I began to understand that I had spent my life going around in circles inside one tiny world, but that there were plenty of other worlds on this earth and whether I liked it or not I wasn't at the center

when the pot reached a boil I poured the scalding water into a sock and black juice came out, as black as coffee but without the taste or the potency, but it was good all the same and at least it warmed the belly

I carried bowls to Henri and Louis, who, when they saw me coming, laid down hammers and nails and shaking their heads sat on the step

"What do you think, Séraphine?"

Henri asked

"About what?"

he swept his arm through the air

"Of this . . . this place we've ended up"

"This land scares me"

I squeezed my eyes shut to block it all out, just long enough for a shiver to run down my spine and my hands to shake and my jaws to clench, as if some mysterious power descended from the heavens or rising from who knows what abyss was trying to put me on guard

"I don't see why"

answered Henri, and he couldn't have been the only one who didn't see why

I gave myself a good shake and opened my eyes to the day's benevolent light, without another word I gathered the bowls, leaving the two men to their labors while I joined my sister, who already had a basin of dirty laundry on her shoulder, I wedged the other against my hip and we fell in line behind the other women who also had laundering to do, they were talking to the soldiers assigned as our escorts, laughing and arching their backs for those boys who couldn't have been more than twenty

"Well, ladies, shall we?"

we were ready though not serene, but one way or another we needed to wash our laundry in the wadi, a

temperamental river that flew into a rage at the slightest storm, so shepherded by six loaded rifles we walked
to the water's edge and knelt in the sand to soak our
shirts and trousers and other shabby garments in the
clear current cascading over the stones, no longer paying any mind to the soldiers whose leader made sure to
keep them at a distance from our tempting derrières

I couldn't help but cast a worried glance at the
mass of rocks and shrubs looming over us, prepared,
in the still air and deceptively kind light that lulled
the senses, to signal the soldiers and their rifles at the
slightest falling rock, twitch of a branch, or fleeting
glint of a yataghan lying in wait, because every one of
us wretched women, I more than the others perhaps,
remembered what had happened to Germaine, who'd
gone by herself to do her laundry telling anyone who
would listen that there wasn't a man or woman alive
who could keep her from her washing, that she'd seen
plenty of good-for-nothings, vagabonds, and cutthroats
and it would take more than some empty-bellied Arab
to scare her

yes, she saw plenty, holy Mary mother of God

a band of raggedy natives attacked her as she rinsed
her sheets, she didn't even have time to turn around
or cry out, it was as if those barbarian dogs had fallen
straight out of Allah's sky, yataghans raised they
stabbed her in the heart and gouged out her eyes, de-
lighted no doubt to watch them roll like marbles in the
sand, then they eviscerated her, she was near split from

throat to groin, and with their savage hands ripped out
her guts inch by bloody inch, and last they cut off her
head, which they must have taken with them because
no one ever found it, hard as we all looked, her husband
and the rest of us, Germaine's head was nowhere to be
seen

holy Mary mother of God

so we had to bury the body without its head, and I
remember how her husband kneeling before the grave
jumped in and embraced the coffin, screaming at the
African heavens that he would kill with his own two
hands the men who had decapitated his wife

"I'll kill them! I'll kill them with my bare hands!"

he swore

two soldiers had to climb down into the grave to
get him, but he was in such a rage that the only way to
bring him back up was to knock him out

the hole was sealed with rocks and dirt atop which
the captain had a wooden cross erected, it was the first
cross in that field chosen as our cemetery, the first cross
for a dead colonist I mean, because two soldiers had
succumbed to their injuries since our arrival but they
had been buried in the plot reserved for the army

but on this day, a clear-skied morning in March, we
calmly returned along the path to the colony, our basins
of clean laundry on our heads to protect us from the
sun, it was hot, the sweat on our backs soaked through
our shirts, our cheeks were red and our lips dry, our
breathless chests heaving, but all the same, one of the

women found the courage to hum a French song that the soldiers marching behind us took up in unison

were our troubles finally over?

the spring light was kindling something in our hearts, new desires ran through our veins like bubbling sap, desires to work the earth, to plant, to harvest, to build, and above all, the desire to please our men and bear them children

once the palisade the soldiers had erected around the colony was in sight, I felt the urge to cry out in joy but I held it in the best I could, one hand on my chest, the other on my stomach, and looking at my sister I noticed that she too was on the verge of tears, that her eyes were glistening the same way mine must have been in that moment

were our troubles finally over?

(BLOODBATH)

We're no angels

the captain's been bellowing that in our ears from the start, and he's bellowing it now

"You're no angels!"

as the sun tumbles behind the horizon and larks emerge from the mastic trees and dwarf palms to criss-cross the sky

"Christ alive! Do you hear me when I tell you you're no angels?!"

as if we were deaf and recruited yesterday, as if we were still stumbling beneath our military gear when the truth is, since landing in Sidi-Ferruch, we've come an awful long way, we've set villages on fire and chopped off heads, rutted at least one hundred thousand females and run through how many hundreds of thousands of barbarians with our bayonets? how many I ask? after fifteen years of conquest in this cursed land, it's hard to keep track

Staouëli, Fort-l'Empereur, Mascara, Constantine, our victorious passage through the Iron Gates as the bugles blazed, the capture of Abd al-Qader's smala, the Dahra smoke-outs

we're no more afraid of the yataghan than we are the roaring of the desert lion that wakes us in the night as we snore like pigs around our campfires, no more afraid of the brain-melting sun than we are the African maladies hell-bent on our demise, the shakes, the runs, camp fever, and mustn't forget the Kabyle worms that'll eat a man's insides and the fanatical winds swirling down from Mahomed's seven heavens to gnaw our wounds to the bone

so take a good look at us, you vermin, you devil spawn, spy on us all you like from inside your gourbis, snickering with fingers pointed at our down-at-the-heel mud hooks and darned trousers and dented shakos, nothing can stop us, will ever stop us, we march like one man through the cutthroat alleys of your towns and villages, we pillage your mosques, casbahs, and graves, in our fury we trample your wheat fields and hack down your orchards, every last orange, olive, lemon, and almond tree, anything that we can use as firewood when we camp under the stars and it grows cold and we need to warm our weary bones, we divert water from your springs to our thirsty gullets, we seize your camels and flocks of sheep, deaf to your girlish whimpers and blind to your grimaces of horror, no, your tears aren't convincing in the least

"You're no angels!"

no, we're no angels, captain, which is why we're still alive, soldiers from sunup to sundown, and in our sleep, too, proud every God-given day to serve France and carry out your orders

except that tonight we can't bear it anymore, the wind's howling and it's cold as a wedge, captain, it's time the troop finds somewhere to spend the night, a shelter with nice thick walls even if those walls are made of bricks of dried mud that let in a draft, it's time to light some fires and warm our tired hides, and eat, captain, anything will do, open our gobs and shove down whatever we can get our hands on, donkey, sheep, camel, the meat doesn't matter, cooked or raw, same difference to us, as long as warm animal blood fills our mouths and breathes life back into our arms and legs weary from too much war

too much plundering, too much man-to-man combat, bayonet versus yataghan

it's time to guzzle some French spirits, for an hour or two forget what we are and what we're becoming, sprawled in the straw or curled up on a rancid pile of blankets that reek of wool grease, letting the brandy-fire do its job deep in our bellies in that secret place where our victims' bodies writhe from a thousand tortures and the primal screams of the men and women speared by our sharpened bayonets echo for eternity amid the heady, musty odor of spilled blood, yes, let the alcohol burn and carry everything away to the blessed vaults of forgotten history

"Halt!"

shouts our captain

"Halt, my brave soldiers!"

and he points at the clouds weighing down the whole sky, leaving so little space between heaven and earth that we wonder whether there's enough room to advance upright or if we'll have to crawl on our elbows through the godforsaken dust stirred up by the wind like a witch's brew

"We won't make it, captain"

"Take a good look, men"

"We don't see anything, captain"

he turns around, preening like a rooster in his seven-league boots that could cross far more distance than that, he gives us a smug smile and then rattles his saber in the air to rouse our cold-addled brains under the kepis pulled down to our ears

"You don't see the village there at the tip of my finger?"

"No, captain"

"Christ alive! have you all gone blind as bats?!"

he swivels back around and advances, his saber swinging side to side, beheading clumps of esparto

"Fall in line, boys, that's where we'll be sleeping tonight, even if all you lot can see is clouds" and we follow his pachyderm boots, rifles on our shoulders, blankets wrapped around our shivering chests, helping the wounded among us walk this final mile that will supposedly bring us to shelter, the cold growing sharper with every step, lashing our eyes and clouding our vision with tears that drip onto our lips with a familiar taste of bitterness

and at last we see it, we see the damned village, it rises and ripples like a mirage through the bitter tears in our stinging eyes, a wild growl rises from our chests, the sound straightens our spines, liberates us from the deadly cold that thought it could best us, hardens like a fist the desire still buried deep in all of us, and what a mad desire it is, we quicken our step and then begin to run, the hardiest among us fast enough to catch a stitch, our rifle bayonets pointed at the village's trembling walls and poorly locked doors and the hostile silence of its narrow streets

all we hear now is our gasps for breath and our mud hooks skittering excitedly on loose stones

"Go on, soldiers! The village is ours!"

screams the captain, beside himself

and we charge, leaving our wounded, mess kits, and gear behind

"No quarter, men! No quarter!"

we charge like wild bulls, heads down and jaws clenched, as doors open and rusty flintlocks take aim at us, sizzling as they spit out lead shot that buzzes like bees around our ears but doesn't slow us any

night falls and with it snowflakes from God knows where

but little matter the night, and little matter the snow, the flintlocks don't have time to fire a second time, we're already upon the men aiming them at our chests, we're already running them through, lifting them off the ground and into the air like pigs on a spit as blood rushes from their gaping bellies, spurts onto the walls, and splatters the terrified faces of the women and children screaming at the top of their lungs

from house to house the screams rise and swell in a thundering chorus of such power it is surely intended to rip the entire village from its earthly roots and carry it far from the malediction of war

enough commentary! we don't want to hear it any more than we want to see the accusatory looks of those who would judge us, and besides, our foray was lightning-quick, no need to make a fuss, not even ten corpses piled up at the village entrance, and as for the women, children, and elderly on their knees begging us not to kill them in their Berber gibberish

"Lā taqtulūnī! lā taqtulūnī!"

we won't, we'll simply kick them out, seeing as we need their houses to make ourselves a fire, eat some fresh meat, and sleep in the warmth

buoyed by victory we race like devils through the alleyways searching the fallen night for anything that glitters, anything that might satiate us, rummaging through trunks for gold, coins, and gems set in necklaces, bracelets, and other baubles for which the merchants in Algiers pay good money, stripping makeshift beds of their blankets and rugs, emptying the silos of sorely missed grain and flour, and the barns, the animals pawing at the ground in fear

the sun's so long gone that indoors the darkness is as thick as ink, gleaming with the panicked eyes of how many sheep? we don't know and we don't need to, however many it's a bargain and the pickings easy, that's the only thing on our minds, and the only thing that excites us, as we maneuver animals between our thighs and with one hand force up their heads and with the other slit their exposed throats

once again blood goes everywhere, it spurts onto our hands, arms, and fraying trousers, and into our eyes and beards, fat red bubbles float into our mouths, and the sensation of hot animal blood trickling down our throats to refortify our insides feels good

no, we're no angels, we're soldiers dammit!

and we soldiers desperately need blood, warm blood, fresh blood, to ward off the shakes and the runs and camp fever, 'cause it works a hell of a lot better than the quinine sulfate being sold for a fortune to the settlers stuck in that putrid swamphole they call Boufarik

"Go on, men, gorge yourselves!"

roars our captain upon his triumphant return from his hunt for female prey, a young catch quaking in terror under his arm we gulp down the blood but there's too much, we feel it oozing out our ears, nostrils, and eyes, it rushes back up our throats and we're forced to spit it out, then piss it out, our bladders tight as drums

"Well then piss it out, men! Piss away!"

orders the captain, who's jammed a second catch under his other arm

we spray the walls with bloody urine, grunting and cussing, then grab our slaughtered sheep by the hooves and drag them through alleys blanketed with snow and howling with wind until we find a house, ten unruly battle-drunk foot soldiers, sometimes fifteen, to a gourbi, most of them without windows or even a second floor

"One sheep per shack! No more!"

we build roaring fires inside the huts, we burn whatever we find, little matter as long as it warms us to the bone, incinerates our crabs and boils and the rest of the filthy vermin nibbling on our balls, higher now! higher! and in the glee spread by the leaping flames we shed our ragged uniforms at last, toss aside our rifles and mud hooks and drop our threadbare trousers and greatcoats, bellies bared to the heaven-sent firelight, we wriggle our paunches, hopping from one foot to the other, arms open to embrace young mademoiselles we can now fondle only in our dreams

"Dance, men! Shake and shimmy the cholera away!"

as whole sheep roast on spits, giving off smoke and a smell of grilled meat so intoxicating that we lose our heads and pounce on the near-raw mutton

"Christ alive!"

our hands rip apart the glistening meat, claim a tail, an ear, a hoof, grab a protruding bone, plunge into the entrails in search of a heart, lung, or liver, then we clamp our greedy jaws around our hard-won trophies, grinding muscle, licking fat, and sucking marrow, down the hatch it goes, the meat descending like a miracle to our innards, filling and swelling our bellies

and still the snow continues to fall, gathering on the shoulders of the women, children, and elderly chased from their homes and forced to wander like lost souls the outskirts of the village now guarded by sentinels bearing rifles, chased from their homes, they go round in circles, trembling from cold, moaning and weeping, seeking shelter but finding none, until finally they take refuge in a copse of bay trees, the women and the elderly bundle the children in their rags and huddle beneath the branches as they wait for the sky to offer a miracle that will not come

enough! enough, I say! pray tell, what miracle is meant to fall from the sky?! if anyone's offering miracles, it's us soldiers, we're the ones ridding this godforsaken country of its fanatics, we're the ones building towns and roads, and drying your cursed swamps, and inventing quinine sulfate, and planting thousands upon thousands of trees to suck up the wretched fumes of this hellhole you call Algeria, so don't you dare reproach us for breaking down a few doors to warm our cold, tired bones, or for slaughtering four, maybe five sheep to fill our empty bellies, on the contrary! let us rest in piece, sprawled on some dry straw or a wool rug as we fill our lungs with smoke from the Turkish tobacco you'll find in every merchant's stall in Algiers

"If our days are to grow ever darker and bloodier, then let the night succumb to all the excesses of our revived bodies, tits bared!"

cry some of the men

"Hip hip! let it crackle and burn!"

respond others

"Paint the night white with jism and muffle its screams!"

add a few others, aroused

at midnight, the captain in his infinite generosity relinquishes the three females he used and abused for much of the night, three pretty young things, stocky and hairy the way we like them in the troop, not wild, resigned to satisfying us because there's no way around it

they're disheveled and trembling, bellies spattered with sperm

"You, what's your name?"

"Zahia"

answers one

"And you?"

"Hayet"

"And you?"

"Maïssa"

mouths pursed and eyes bold despite the captain's repeated onslaughts, they open their legs for us sixty times so the troop's sixty soldiers can forget their troubles and with broad thrusts clear a path through the calcinated forests of their Bedouin bush

and only when dawn is well on its way do we collapse onto the straw and makeshift beds, drunk, sated, balls finally emptied of the primal urges that were an unrelenting torture during our endless battles, our forced marches, our illnesses

"Christ alive, that does a man good!"

does a man good to forget everything, to sprawl naked atop a woman's loins and fall asleep in her heat, intoxicated to madness by her soft and bitter breath, coddled in the dampness of her thighs, surrendering to her soft witchlike hands

"Do you like your mean little soldier?"

we whisper in their ears

but can these girls truly like these men lumbering on top of them? who forced them to accept the burning seed of their soldier's barbarism?

what a question! not another word, you hear me? leave us be, we're the ones holding the rifles, we're the ones marching for hours along roads lousy with traps, we're the ones dying of camp fever and cholera, so let us enjoy our victories down to the tips of our whistles

"Go on, Zahia, and Hayet, and you too, Maïssa, tell your mean little soldiers you love us"

and that tremulous, terrified love, but love all the same, lulls us to sleep, snoring like hippopotamuses and grunting like bears in our musky sweat, and who cares if it's bone-splitting cold on the hills and in the ravines, for once it's us who are warm atop our straw and our pallets

"for once, Christ alive!"

and when the sun rises at last, when it's time to pull on our trousers, lace up our mud hooks, and shoulder our rifles, we don't spare a glance to the three females huddled up in their rags, it's cold, there's nothing hot to drink, and the march to the fonduk will be long, best to save our strength and munitions for the devils who'll be trying by any means possible to cut off our heads

the soldiers assemble at the village entrance and at the captain's orders, get back on the road, slipping with every step in the frozen snow, which fell for much of the night and buried in deathly silence everything that was familiar to them, they've lost their bearings but little matter, their captain's up ahead, it suffices to follow

and with heavy, crunching steps, the troop fades into the distance

and the crows and dogs return to the village, and in the wake of the crows and dogs, so do the three girls

in a daze they wander the narrow streets calling out to their sisters and brothers, their mothers, their uncles and aunts, and their elders whom they've known since childhood as their protectors from all that is frightening

"Where are you, Old Rahima? where are you?"

they shout until they're hoarse

"Old Dhohra?"

they stumble in the snow, they fall, they graze their knees

"Old Bachir?"

but despite all their efforts, despite combing the village three times over and searching the surroundings, no one answers them, and it's only once the sun sets that they discover in a tangle of bay trees sagging beneath the snow the intertwined bodies of those who the night before had still been their sisters and their brothers, their mothers, their uncles and their aunts, their elders whom they'd known since childhood as their protectors from all that is frightening and who are now nothing but corpses frozen for eternity by a cold winter's night.

(HANDS OF TOIL)

The joy of having a makeshift roof over our heads, though there was nothing grand about it, buoyed our spirits

everywhere you looked the men had a saw or hammer in hand, and our steady labors were proof enough that not one soul had the intention of giving up, for two months settlers and soldiers joined efforts to finish the palisade erected as a rampart between our homes and the cruelty of those who wanted nothing more than to chop off our heads

the evenings were so beautiful, the light so gentle in the sky and here on earth, that Rosette, Célestine, and I got into the habit of walking the whole length of the fence while our five children took advantage of the momentary freedom to run and tussle, buzzing around the soldiers on watch

"Nicolas! François! go play elsewhere!"

we would trade camp gossip, more than happy to have no part in stories that served only to ruin a woman's reputation, though we still snickered as we pointed our own fingers, without proof, at this or that trollop said to sell her body to the soldiers

a large pole had been erected high above the rooftops and the palisade to wave the French flag, a swathe of new, exquisite cloth that was a symbol of our fair claim and one at which we glanced often in the hope that it would keep the dangers sufficiently at bay, the desert lions and horned vipers but most of all the bloodthirsty savages observing our colony from a distance, prepared to leap out of the darkness and slit us nose to navel

once night fell we would make our way home, refreshed by the wind descending from the mountains, and pass on our way a tavern built from the ground up by a man named Gaston Frick, an Alsatian by origin and tough as a boar, who had decided he would make his fortune on African land and in a few weeks' time had nailed some rough-hewn planks into a makeshift counter from behind which he sold brandy, absinthe, and lousy wine from Bône

that was where we often found our men, exhausted from the day's labor of sawing, planing, and nailing planks into a table, bench, or shelves, fortifying a fence or enlarging a shed

and at night, in the light of our lantern and a fire, we would eat a ragout that was simply a mix of whatever the soldiers had brought back from Bône, potatoes,

rice, and cheap cuts of meat that were hard to chew, and
then go to bed candle in hand, I would kiss my daughter
and my two sons

"Sleep tight"

Snuggling together, they would grab my hand

"Mama, are we going to stay here long?"

they asked, brows arched in curiosity

I didn't answer, stroking their heads one last time
before joining Henri under a sheet that hid our bodies
but didn't allow us to do what a husband and a wife do
when they're together in a bed, I stopped Henri's hand
slipping between my thighs

"No, we shouldn't"

"Well the others do"

"No, they don't"

and then we would eventually fall asleep

but this period I'm describing didn't last long, two
months I said, maybe less, for time in Africa isn't mea-
sured as in Europe, it stretches out in a way unfamiliar
to us, and it was during that stretching of time, which
we were just beginning to master, that the heat struck,
pouring over our colony like melted lead, the air outside
and inside our sad wooden shacks became unbreathable, the sun heavy on our shoulders, grinding away our
desire to work, sapping us of our strength, hands limp
and legs shaky, we were forced to spend half the day
in the shade, sitting in the dust with our eyes closed,
hoping that a breath of mountain wind would put some
color back in our drawn faces

but no respite came, holy Mary mother of God

on the contrary, ever hotter waves of fire swept over our cabins, charring in an instant the leaves of the first tomato plants planted by some in the hope of a first harvest before summer, scorching the skin on our faces and hands, burning our retinas, drying our insides until our bellies turned hard as rock

and in such conditions, many fell ill, high fevers confined men and women to their beds, children too, by the dozens, along with the soldiers assigned to keep watch all day along the fence but who couldn't endure the African sun

the captain had no choice but to summon a military doctor who arrived from Bône in such a state that they had to pour two buckets of cool well water over his head and a tall glass of brandy down his throat

soon right as rain he told us

"It's bad all over"

then rolled up his shirtsleeves and continued

"Cholera is ravaging the region. It's in Bône and tomorrow it will be here"

the captain took action immediately, you can't reproach the man for doing nothing, orders were given not to let anyone else enter the colony, the entry gates were closed and we were told to see only our family members and stay away from everyone else

but it was too late, because it was the military doctor himself who brought us the cholera, the night of his arrival he wasn't feeling well, it got so bad he had to lie down in the tent the captain had designated for him and for one hour he battled terrible colic and then he began to vomit, emptied of any remaining strength, he died that night and the soldiers hurriedly carried him to the cemetery by lantern light and tossed him in a hole so his body wouldn't contaminate other bodies

pointless precaution because the next day it was the daughter from the neighboring house, a fourteen-year-old girl, who died, and late in the afternoon her father

holy mother of God

and the mother, who often came with us to do the washing at the banks of the wadi, shot out of her house like a madwoman, pulling her hair, shouting and screaming every insult she could think of at the Lord, she rolled in the dust, scratched her cheeks until they bled, and then forced the soldiers to open the fence gates, and once they were open she ran straight toward the mountains, never turned around, never stopped, and disappeared behind the veil of heat

her name was Marguerite and no one ever knew what became of her

two coffins had to be constructed, father and daughter buried, and it was Gaston Frick who improvised the eulogy, railing in his raspy voice against the misfortune that always targeted the weakest

"Is it fair that tragedy struck a poor family whose sole desire was to till the seven hectares France gave it in peace? I ask this of you, who have only your hands to defend yourselves" dry-mouthed and short-winded, he paused to catch his breath in the choking heat, giving each of us a hard look as he studied our sad, sweating faces

"Will there never be justice on this earth then?"

and I said to myself that "justice" was a word invented by the rich to appease the anger of the poor, but that if you thought hard about it, justice didn't exist, that we ought to learn to live without it and accept the fate reserved by God for every human being who sets foot on this earth.

○

For three days we believed we could escape the ravages of cholera, since the burials of Marguerite's husband and daughter no other case had been signaled in the village

I kept my three children shut inside our house, terrorized same as my sister by the thought that the disease might strike our family, and Célestine watched over her two boys just as keenly, most of the time the children were sleeping on sweat-drenched pallets, and when they weren't asleep, Rosette and I would tell them stories, stories from back home about princesses losing their way in vast forests full of wolves and ogres

Henri and Louis were the only ones to go out, handkerchiefs across the bottom halves of their faces, keeping their distance from anyone they crossed, they would gather news at the tavern, collect some food, and return at sundown telling us there was no need to be afraid, that no one else within the colony walls had been afflicted, and that the captain was doing everything in his power to control the situation

"And in Bône?"

"He heard it's a nightmare there"

And in the unbreathable night air, I told myself there wasn't a ghost of a chance that the colony would escape the epidemic, no chance that this disease that had shown pity for no man would show us any, I was certain—I would have bet my life on it—that its design was to go after our families, so instead of sleeping I prayed with all my strength that God would intervene with his divine power, which protects the good and abandons the evil to their fate

"O Lord, I beg of you, hear my prayer, since the day I was born I haven't asked you for much, I have never in any way abused your power, I have always been humble and obedient, I've lived all my born days by your rules, on the pew with the rest of your flock come Sunday, I never missed a mass or a tithe, not one, so aren't I in my rights to ask you for a favor? O Lord, I beg of you, descend from your heavenly heights, bestow your generosity on me and all in this colony, I beg of you, save us"

and unable to fall asleep, fearful my prayer wouldn't be heard, I waited for the first glimmer of dawn

three days, I said, for three days we hoped for a miracle, when all those three days did was strengthen the powers of a disease I imagined as a wild beast lurking on the other side of the fence that, sick of waiting, chose the morning of the fourth day to pounce on our families, sink its fangs in our weakened flesh, and swallow whole our pitiful little lives

Henri had just opened the door to let in the daylight, I was heating water in a pot, birds were chirping on rooftops cooled by the night winds, when suddenly we heard a scream that turned my blood to ice, Henri looked at me as if the sky was falling on his head

"I'll go see"

"Don't go out there, Henri"

but he was already running toward the tavern, I closed the door and Rosette and Louis, who had jumped out of bed, asked me what was happening

"It's the cholera"

I told them

"Are you sure?"

said Rosette

"Henri went to find out, but I'm sure"

the children were still asleep when Henri came back to tell us that a man had died in the night, that two children and two women were losing the fight for their lives, and that another man across the village also felt very ill

"What are we going to do?"

asked Rosette biting her nails and pacing in circles as if she was losing her wits, and surely willing to pursue any folly that might save the lives of her loved ones

"Calm down, Rosette"

"I can't"

I slipped my arm around her waist and squeezed her tight, my poor sister was trembling, my sister who was usually so strong was so frightened she couldn't stop trembling, and I couldn't blame her because I set to trembling too in spite of myself, so many quivers running down my spine I lost my balance

the four of us sat around the table and drank large bowls of roasted barley in silence, the sunshine entering the room through the cracks in the poorly hung door wasn't sufficient, so Louis had lit a lantern and in the flickering light we stared down at our steaming bowls, not daring to lift our bowed heads and risk meeting someone's gaze, unwilling to see our own fear, the instinctive terror of any flesh-and-blood creature under threat, reflected in their eyes

"The captain asked the carpenters and anyone else who knows their way around a hammer to gather at the workshop to build coffins, he expects lots of folks will die in the coming days"

Henri finally said

he was walking his large fingers across his sunburnt forehead as if they had the power to quiet the dark thoughts sending his head, and mine, and my sister's and brother-in-law's, into a spin

"What are we going to do, Henri?"

I searched his eyes for a reassuring answer but rack his brains though he did, there was no point, he knew perfectly well that he wouldn't find the words to ease my worries and slow my heart racing inside my chest, slow all our hearts, because I had no trouble imagining the same was true of Rosette, and Louis too, who was forcing himself to act like a man, and it was Louis who answered me

"There's nothing to be done, nothing at all, the cholera means our colony is isolated from the rest of the world, no one can enter and no one can leave"

"So we're all going to die?"

asked Rosette

"Of course we're not, we're going to do what's within our means to make sure the cholera doesn't enter our home, we'll keep the door shut, plug the gaps in the walls, drink boiled water, and only eat cooked food"

and just as Louis's common sense was kindling a faint hope that we might fight to stay alive, as if our paltry human efforts had any chance at all of staying the devastating scythe in our midst, someone knocked at our door

"Can I speak to you?"

it was Célestine looking for news, so I answered

"Come in and close the door quick"

she wanted to know how many people were sick and how many people were dead, and I told her that at least six souls had already been taken without the slightest struggle

"I was certain the cholera wouldn't stop with Marguerite's family, and it's not because we had no deaths for three days that we should have thought ourselves safe, my father keeps telling me we should run, take advantage when it gets dark and leave the colony"

"And go where, Célestine?"

"That's what I tell him, go where? some other village that is or soon will be as overrun as ours? but he doesn't want to hear it"

her hands were at her throat and she had a lost look in her eyes, wild almost

"Just what does your father think? that he can use the roads as he pleases? he won't make it one league before he gets his head split by a yataghan"

Henri told her

"Sit down, Célestine, and have some coffee with us"

she sat at one end of the bench as I poured what was left of the pot into a bowl

"Drink, it'll do you good"

then we went quiet, each of us stewing in thoughts we'd have rather not voiced before the others.

○

And without so much as a by-your-leave, without a chance to voice the slightest protest, we settlers who had done no wrong were plunged into the flames of a hell barely imaginable

a hell that in my woman's naiveté I had believed confined to the bowels of the earth, under the dominion of the devil and his demons wielding deadly pitchforks, but which I saw with my own eyes emerge from

the wicked depths to overrun the earth and sow terror, to vanquish our colony and with broad swings of
its scythe cut down men, women, and children inside
their wooden cabins, and this in utter impunity—hear
me well, I say utter impunity—for never did heaven and
its divine representatives intervene

holy Mary mother of God, why did you abandon us?

never came to our aid to douse the flames consuming us

at least tell me why

never lifted a finger to stop the scythe blade at our
throats

yes, tell me why, at least.

○

All the following day, and the day after that and the
remaining days of the week, people died in the sun's
blistering heat before they could even realize what was
happening, they would leave their cabins, taking care
to walk along the walls in the shade, to relieve themselves in the public latrines or draw a bucket of water
or toss out their waste, they would take ten, twenty
steps and then collapse in the dust in a fit of vomit-
ing and diarrhea, after which, emptied of their insides,
they died surrounded by a cloud of flies that wasted no
time buzzing into their mouths and ears, then all that
remained for the soldiers on interminable patrol to do
was collect the bodies and make them disappear within

the four planks of a lopsided coffin on which was etched
a surname or sometimes no name at all

and for those who died at home it was even more
terrible, their families howling in pain at seeing a loved
one pass so violently, the afflicted would grasp at an
outstretched hand or a face leaning over them, but
there was nothing to be done, their bodies writhing
in agony seemingly wrenched away by some invisible
force, torn from life and the living to be tossed into the
bubbling cauldrons of the kingdom of the dead

five or six times a day amid the deadly silence that
had overtaken the colony, tarnishing the blue sky,
crushing our roofs and chests, robbing us of breath, five
or six times a day, and often more, the fence gates had
to be opened to let out coffins carried on men's shoulders all the way to the cemetery where they were buried before weeping families on their knees in the dust,
heads lowered to avoid the sun's blinding rays

and it was on the night of the sixth day that
Louis, after making coffins from sunrise to sunset,
came home so tired that he skipped dinner and went
straight to bed

"What's wrong, Louis?"

asked Rosette in a panic

he didn't answer, simply turned his head and looked
at Rosette as though he was struggling to put a name
to the face of the woman perched over him, all the hu-
manity fading from his eyes, which were sinking deeper

into their sockets, then he opened his mouth like a fish
out of water and stuck out a gritty tongue

"He's thirsty!"

Rosette rushed to fetch what remained of the boiled
water, poured it into a glass, and kneeled beside her
husband

"Drink, my dear, drink, it will make you feel better"

she lifted Louis's head and forced him to drink as
Henri and I tried to rub some life back into the with-
ered skin of his hands and feet

I had shut the three children inside the bedroom
and I could hear them asking

"Mama, why did you shut us in?"

"To protect you"

"Protect us from what?"

"Louis is sick, you mustn't go near him"

"Does he have the cholera?"

asked François

"Answer us, Mama, does he have the cholera?"

"I don't know"

and then Louis started to vomit, and after the vom-
iting he had terrible diarrhea, Rosette couldn't bear
to watch, she left the cabin, shaking with sobs, and I
had no choice but to follow her to make sure she didn't
fall, helping her down the three front steps, then helping her to sit herself down on the ground against the
wooden wall, I took my poor sister in my arms, pressed
her tear-drenched face to my bosom, and embraced her
tightly as if it was in my power to ease her pain

above us the black desert sky was spangled with stars and a cool mountain breeze was whirling gleefully over the rooftops, as if that sky, those stars, and that breeze had never considered the misfortune of men on this earth

and after a while, perhaps a long while, Rosette had nodded off, Henri opened the door and sat down on the step, stuffed and lit his pipe before drawing puffs of tobacco into lungs that sorely needed it

Rosette started awake and asked

"Well? any better?"

staring straight ahead, Henri answered

"He's dead."

○

Two men came knocking at our door, they lifted the plain wood coffin with Louis inside to their shoulders and carried it to the cart that was used to transport the dead, and then we, I mean poor Rosette, Henri, Célestine, and I, took our places in the line of people accompanying the departed, there were seven or eight coffins already, the horse was surely straining to pull the cart in that heat, which was already unbearable early though it was, and as I supported my sister, who had a handkerchief over her face, I watched that horse walk, I watched its muscles twitch beneath its coat and its ears endlessly flick away flies

armed soldiers kept guard before and behind the procession, ready to intercede at the slightest alarm the horse stopped when we reached the cemetery, each family carried its coffin to the spot it had chosen and the hole it had dug, Henri had done the digging for Rosette's husband, he dug and shoveled a good part of the night, returning at dawn and sleeping only two or three hours before washing up and following us to the cemetery, shovel in one hand and ropes in the other

there was an acacia tree near our hole, which is where we huddled to muster our strength, mopping the sweat from our brows, Rosette looked around at the graves and crosses that had multiplied in only eight days

"He didn't want us to come"

she finally said

she had stopped crying, judging no doubt that given the tragedy in our midst, there was no point feeling sorry for herself, instead she clenched her fists and furiously bit into the knots of her handkerchief

"Let's make haste, Rosette, the soldiers won't allow us much time"

"I know"

Henri signaled that he and I should lower the coffin but Rosette stepped between us

"It should be me"

she took the rope from my hands and then it was she and Henri who lowered Louis to the bottom of the grave, after which the four of us got on our knees and prayed in silence, palms joined against our wretched chests

Henri stood first, he grabbed his shovel and tossed onto the coffin a spadeful of dirt that echoed in the silence like a clap of thunder or else a gavel hammering down

holy Mary mother of God, what did we do to deserve such cruel punishment?

Célestine and I made the sign of the cross but not Rosette, she stood and turned her back to the hole that Henri was filling, walked alone between the mounds of dirt and stone stretching out one beside the other, then Célestine and I caught up to her and gently wrapped our arms around my poor sister, wandering with her among those buried bodies like three wailers fresh out of tears, faces to the sun and battling the sudden sirocco that was lifting our skirts and rustling our mourning corsages

at the soldiers' summons we left the cemetery, one family behind the other, all gaunt from fatigue, all consumed by the fear of what would befall us tomorrow (and what could befall us now that hell had opened beneath our feet?), meanwhile another cart pulled by another horse and followed by another column of people with tear-stricken faces was getting in line to take our place on the rocky ground

holy Mary mother of God

and that night, like every night of the week since the new army doctor had run out of home remedies and found nothing better to suggest than that we dance until the blood boiled in our arteries and our bodies sweated out the poison, can you imagine! but such was our fear of dying that we obeyed, and on that grim night following the burial we left our five children with Célestine's father, and she, Rosette, Henri, and I, exhausted though we were from the heat and the day's sadness, went to dance at the tavern where Gaston Frick had hired an accordion player and for a few coins promised us a proper soiree with proper spirits from sundown to sunup

and what a sight we made joylessly dancing those waltzes and polkas, flesh-and-bone ghosts step-hopping around other flesh-and-bone ghosts, warming our blood until we turned crimson, sweating out our miseries until the accordion player's fingers began to ache and the man decided to go to bed

we took the doc's advice as if it was the word of God, our legs turned to jelly and our eyelids felt heavier than iron but we didn't succumb to the fatigue, the cholera needed scaring off, it needed to be kept from entering our bodies by any means possible, and if by misfortune the sickness had entered us at some point during the day, then we'd expunge it from every pore on our bodies by waltzing like raving loons

I don't know how many nights we danced to an accordion that for sure didn't sound the way it used to, we skipped and spun without listening to the notes because the instrument didn't seem much like an accordion at all, but rather a bell ringing the death knoll from dusk to dawn to remind us of the terrible truth of our human lives that had only ever been and always would be hanging by a thread

woe upon us

no I don't know how many nights we lost our minds in the smoke and steam that filled Gaston's tavern, and I won't tell you how many settlers ended up in the cemetery, resting for all eternity within four planks of cheap wood

soon enough our grave, above which Henri had planted a cross with Louis's surname

CALLOT

soon enough our grave got bigger to make room for our two sons, who passed in a way I'd rather not say, seeing how words are powerless to describe the suffering of our two boys, who only ever wanted to enjoy the life Henri and I had given them

holy Mary mother of God, you've torn out half of my heart

and hands trembling with despair Henri made two more crosses on which he wrote in black paint

NICOLAS JOUHAUD & FRANÇOIS JOUHAUD

did I leave anything out?

oh yes, our poor Célestine lost her father and one of her sons, then there was just her left in the cabin, her tall body bent under the weight of her grief and her youngest boy, Gérard, who wasn't yet ten

did I leave anything out?

just this

one morning, the raging maw of hell that had been devouring us for weeks suddenly snapped shut and the cholera disappeared, abandoning us to our fate

the houses, open once again, were cleaned and redistributed, for many of them had lost all their inhabitants, and those of us who had survived tried to enjoy life again but was it possible? surely not, our doleful eyes and sunken chests and hair grayed by suffering proved as much day in and day out, and the captain who gathered us to speak of the future had a hard time making himself heard, meekly we listened to his words, meekly we nodded our heads, but we had lost our bearings, not to mention our souls or nearly, and the feeling prevented us from resuming the daily labors that we had abandoned, from finding true meaning for our presence on this godforsaken Algerian land

hell had disappeared but we weren't ready to forget that it was there, beneath our bare feet treading the ground in all ignorance, and that at any moment the chasm could open again and do with our lives what it wanted, without our God being stirred in the slightest— though we'd been praising him without fail for centuries

how can one believe, after that?

(BLOODBATH)

"Attack, my brave soldiers!"

because it's Christmas and we have to take shelter somewhere, the captain points his saber at the fonduk and its tails of acrid black chimney smoke spread by the winds of Allah that have been tormenting us for weeks

"Attack!"

we know it's Christmas, captain, Breton, Alsatian, or Marseillais, we all know that tomorrow night marks the birth of the baby Jesus, which will be celebrated by every church in France with due pomp, and even if there's nothing very Catholic about our soldier hearts and minds, even if, as you're always reminding us, my captain, we're no angels, we still want to feel the warmth of a fire on our balls for Christmas, warm balls and full bellies

and with a rage more Christian than usual we attack the fonduk, pupils dilated, nostrils twitching, and teeth bared like fangs, we rush through the archway, bayonets forward, and impale the hell devils in our path as they raise their so-called pacifist arms to the sky, cries trapped in their throats, as our captain fells two or three devils himself

then, silence

there's nothing left to impale, nothing to decapitate, the survivors are on their knees, foreheads against the ground, praying that we spare their flea-ridden sacks of flesh, the captain's pacing the courtyard in his seven-league boots, hair akimbo on his battle-roused scalp, he inspects some frightened camels in one corner, a mare's nest of crates and rugs in another, circles back to our captives kneeling in prayer and shouts

"Shut your potato traps, goddammit!"

his saber swoops over their heads, it whistles with rage in the trembling light as he stomps between the burnooses sprawled in the mud, submissive as dogs

"At my feet and quiet about it!"

now our captain's strutting, thirty Arabs crawl to him, prepared to lick his boots, their submission pleases him, he relishes it, one sharp eye on us as we snicker behind our scabby beards

"Who's in charge here?"

"I am, sidi...commander, sir"

an old Arab stands

"Son of a bitch! did I tell you to get up?"

"No, sidi-commander"

"On your knees, then!"

the man kneels, eyes downcast like a beaten dog, and crosses his hands on his chest

"Now, seeing how you speak a little French, if you can call it that, you ought to be able to tell me how many rebels you're hiding in your gourbis"

"I hide nothing, sidi-commander, may Allah the All-Mighty cut off my tongue if I lie"

"Is that so? well may he cut off your balls while he's at it, because I know you're lying, dammit! and I'm not a man to lie to, believe you me"

"I do not lie"

"I know your kind, you and those hyenas of yours that sink their bloody fangs into my poor soldiers who've come all the way from France to pacify your god-damned country and clean it of its vermin, Christ alive! and this is how you thank us?"

he chokes on his words, insides curdling from rage, his ears red, which is a bad sign indeed, then our captain clears his throat and spits fuming gobs of phlegm

"How about I slice this old lecher open? reach into his guts and pull out the warm, blood-soaked truth that the bastard won't tell me himself, the miserable son of a dog!"

the saber twirls above the old man's head, ready to carry out the verdict that will come any moment now, and we're thinking we'll have to add another head to the captain's count, which means he might find himself tied with our current decapitation champion, Lepéreux, that Alsatian pig who never misses a chance to show off his skill with a blade

"Have pity, sidi-general"

"It's commander!"

"Sidi-commander...have pity for my brothers and myself, hand on my heart I tell you again that we are friends of France and you won't find those who seek to kill you here"

"You sure about that?"

"Yes, sidi-commander, I am sure"

against all expectations our captain sheathes his saber and crosses his arms over his chest

"For once I want to believe you, son of Mahomed, let this be my way of celebrating Christmas, believing you and sparing your life, because where I'm from, on Christmas Day we have the custom of forgiving any who have slighted us, no, no, don't give me those hound dog black-as-sin eyes, you're already making me want to draw my saber again"

the Arab throws himself on the ground, stroking and kissing the captain's pachyderm boots until he gets a hard kick to the rear and rolls into the mud

"I'll spare every one of you sons of Mahomed, the grandsons too, I'll spare every one of you raggedy devils more full of shit than a pigpen, but only on one condition, you hear me? just one, which is that you serve me and my entire troop without fail until we leave, which won't be anytime soon, I may as well tell you now that we'll be spending the winter in the fonduk, and for however long it lasts, you'll need to make us food so we can eat when we're hungry and fetch us straw so we can sleep when we're tired and women so we can fornicate when the fancy for some horizontal refreshments strikes us"

"Women, sidi-commander?"

"Yes, let's say a handful of well-shaped moukère wenches, if you get my meaning?"

"No, sidi-commander, there is no one here but our wives and our daughters and our sons"

"And where might they all be?"

"Hiding in the gourbis"

the daylight is fading, swallowed by foreboding clouds, and the endlessly howling wind has abruptly cooled, turning our feet to ice, curse this country! if it wasn't for our captain we'd have run these savages through a long time ago and occupied their huts, what's the point of prattling on with a Bedouin whose only thought is to cut off your balls?

"Lepéreux, take four men and fetch me the women" orders the captain

Lepéreux obeys, saber drawn and soldiers in tow, the quintet overjoyed to stir up the pot, and they fetch them all right, every moukère in the fonduk, the most docile ones wrapped up in their veils and whimpering with fear, their brats tight in their arms, while those who kick and spit in the soldiers' faces get dragged in by their hair, shoved to the ground, and beaten near unconscious

"Here they are, captain"

Lepéreux stands at attention, eyes bright and lips glistening with bestial saliva as he waits for orders that don't come, the captain's busy inspecting the flock of females, he rips off veils, pinches cheeks, sticks a probing finger into mouths of venomous teeth

"Why, your women are fit and fine! you're lucky, truly! you won't find ones like these in the French provinces, ours are all pox-ridden and down-at-the-heel from working the fields and popping out babies!"

we use our rifles to hide the peals of laughter we feel rising in our bellies, wouldn't take much to have us in stitches

"Christ alive! these sons of Mahomed aren't bothered at all"

and casual as can be, he fondles a breast here, a rear end there

"You've got to squeeze it to believe it!"

except our captain couldn't imagine that the Arabs would dare get jealous, he forgot about their pathological pride, so then, of course, a one-eyed fellow with filthy curly hair rises from the group of kneeling men and charges him yataghan raised

"Look out!"

shouts Lepéreux

and our captain spins around before the one-eyed brute reaches him, with one swipe of his saber he slices off the man's hand, with another, his head, a clean cut, flawless, and the blood spurts, and the women cry out, and the kneeling Arabs dig their nails into the palms of their impotent fists

"Son of a bitch!"

roars the captain

the man's a lion, which is why we're proud to call him our captain

"Those are our women, sidi-general"

"Commander!"

"Yes, sidi-commander"

"What were you about to say, old man?"

"I say that these are our women, and that in this country, we don't touch another man's woman"

the captain wipes his saber on a fold of his trousers, with one twitchy hand pushes his hair back

"Did I not say that you need to serve me and my troop without fail? did I not warn you that I would only spare your heads on the condition that you meet our every desire? for food and beds of fresh straw and your women for fornicating with?"

"That is not possible, sidi-commander"

"What isn't possible?"

"Screwing our women, they are our women, they belong to us, it is Allah who gave them to us and Allah the All-Mighty does not allow other men to make use of them"

"Think hard, old man, think hard about what I'm about to say and open wide your cussed simpleton eyes"

"They are open, sidi-commander"

"I have taken your fonduk with the steel of my bayonets and my saber and I'm the master now, the master
supreme who gets to decide who lives and who dies, in-
cluding you, and you there, and you"

at that he slides his thumb across his neck as though
he's ready to behead each of the men at whom he
pointed with his saber

"I give my soldiers the order and all your men are
done for, old, young, makes no difference, poof, you'll
all disappear, and your women you're refusing to give
up will belong to me and my men anyway, you don't
have a choice, old man"

the Arab closes his eyes and wrings his hands in the
folds of his burnoose, muttering prayers into his beard
and paying no heed to our captain's threats

"You don't believe me, is that it? you think that my
commanding officers in Algiers didn't give me free reign
to cut off your murderous heads whenever I like? well
you are mistaken, for ten years now I've been looting
your villages and burning your fields, killing any man
who resisted and raping his women, that's my job as a
soldier, I'm given what I need to get it done, and when
I report victory they send me congratulations from Algiers and Paris, so it's not thirty louse-ridden savages
living in a fonduk in the middle of some godforsaken
desert that are going to disobey my orders, you understand me, old man?"

"They are our women, sidi-commander"

says the Arab, daring to raise his head and meet the captain's gaze

"Christ alive! he's busting my chops, isn't he?! this old jackal is sitting cozy in his babouches having a good laugh while here I am wasting my spit trying to explain how war works"

then our captain raises his saber again and slams it down on the old man's throat, the head rolls into the mud as the body momentarily remains on its knees, blood gushing

"Christ alive!"

which is their signal, thirty Arabs reach into their burnooses to pull out thirty yataghans and charge us shrieking in fury, but what do these sons of Mahomed expect? they think they're going to scare us? our rifles up just as quick, we shove our sharpened bayonet blades into their bellies and we don't hold back, we slice, we stab, we spear that Mahomedan meat until it's mush, there are cries and screams from every direction but we don't hear a sound, it's raining blood, our greatcoats drenched, but we don't see a drop

it's true, we're no angels

but do we need angels to pacify these barbarian lands?

"No, my captain, we don't need angels! we need soldiers and not just any, we need the kind of soldiers who fear nothing!"

○

Then it's another gray and dirty day, the sky heavy with the uncustomary weight of clouds that look as if they've escaped from the darkest of African abysses

the captain, who rose before everyone, gives his orders, we line up before him half-awake, coats and shakos sloppy, our bodies crawling with gourbi vermin, tired and saddle-sore from mounting resigned moukères all night long

he wants us to clear the corpses, clean up the courtyard, and stash our kits in the huts

"Manners, men! we're stuck in this rathole of a fonduk for two months at least, so let's see some discipline and organization, goddammit! get to scrubbing now, I want this place gleaming like a French whore's tits under a full moon"

he gives us a stern look as he strides across the courtyard, stepping over the bodies in disgust

"Hop to!"

we click our heels and salute our captain as he returns to a squat gourbi he's claimed as his makeshift watchtower, on the roof we can see he's hoisted the French flag and how our spirits are lifted by those three colors proudly shining amid a desert of grays

in the days that follow we drag the corpses far from the fonduk and pile them near the wadi in the hope that the desert lions, along with the hyenas, jackals, and vultures, will lose no time cleaning up for us, then we turn to the blackish pools of blood in the courtyard, which we fill with shovelfuls of dirt and rocks, we scrub the doors splattered with stains, we sluice down the gourbi where three women who refused to submit stabbed themselves in the heart, and finally we light a fire in the middle of the courtyard to burn the soiled straw, louse-ridden rags, and anything else of no utility to us

we toil until nightfall, and when the sun sets we warm our hides around our fires, aching muscles revived by the couscoussou prepared by our moukères as we drink the brandy our captain never forgets to bring on our expeditions

"Brandy makes good soldiers, isn't that right, men?"

says our captain, seated like a pasha on a throne of carved wood that he found in the watchtower, which he uses to give his orders and set his law on the flock of moukères

we nod, because deep down we know he's right, that we wouldn't fight so hard in battle if we didn't have our slug of alcohol igniting a fire in our brains

the nights are clear and still, the northern wind has died down, and the jumble of stars hanging above our heads is like a benediction, divine grace sent from a heaven with which we feel reconciled, and maybe we're no angels but some nights we come close to wishing we were

"Isn't that right, captain?"

it's his turn to nod, his chosen moukère sitting on his knee, a Berber with crazed eyes whom the rest of us don't dare approach, Aïcha she's called, a mountain gazelle not even twenty and she's all his, no question he's intending to fully avail himself during our two months of hibernation, he beheaded her father but she doesn't blame him, or else the treacherous creature is simply pretending not to and biding her time, and it seems to us that our captain is playing along, waiting like us for her to betray him so he can cut off her head

Lepéreux parceled out the women old enough to spread their legs, he found a couple dozen between fifteen and fifty, which makes one moukère for every three or four soldiers, which isn't too bad, one day it's him, next day it's you, there's no squabbling, no fisticuffs, in any case the captain has his eye on us

this barracks life heals our wounds, no more slogging empty-bellied along trails of dust and mud, we can shit and piss in peace, safe from the Kabyle ruffians always itching to cut off our balls, we eat our fill from the stores in the fonduk, we hunt hares and antelopes for some variety, then we set our rifles and bayonets on the shelf and fancy ourselves masons or carpenters with the means on hand, we play ruthless card games for hours around braziers whenever it rains or snows, and whenever the rain or snow is so heavy that we're forced to stay inside the gourbis and brood more of the vermin always crawling up our asses

we do our best hunting in the snow, when a good three or four feet fall in a single night and all of sudden this wretched land disappears, miraculously elbowed out of the way by a naked horizon pure of all sin and deceit,

there are ten of us who wake awestruck to that blanket
of light and silence spread by some higher power that
we soldiers doing the devil's work would rather know
nothing about, it takes us a few minutes rubbing our
gummed-up eyes and clearing the wax from our ears
to believe it, and then there's ten of us pulling on our
fraying trousers and our mud hooks, we grab our rifles
and rush out into the snow, Raymond, the fellow from
Nantes, in the lead because the man's never missed a racing hare, he can take down a gazelle at a hundred paces
with a single rifle shot

and sinking in snow up to our knees it almost feels
as if we're back home, as if we're kids again bundled
in our mufflers and roaming the streets of our home-
towns, tears in our eyes from joy and from cold, hurling
our devilish snowballs through a stagecoach window or
at some moneybag in a fancy fur cap, under the swirling
capelets of giggling schoolgirls

"What do you see, Raymond?"

"Shut up, you sods!"

our Raymond is kneeling, rifle up, so we imitate
him, looking around for what might have alerted him,
we don't see anything but clusters of dwarf palms
posted like sentinels in the field of snow, so we wait,
laboring to hide our breath white from the cold behind
the sleeves of our greatcoats

and then a hare comes hurtling from behind a palm
tree and hops across the snow, scuttling, weaving,
jumping so high it's near flying, and we tell ourselves

that an animal like that doesn't give a toss about rifles, whether it's Raymond or us sods taking aim, that nothing can stop that damned jackrabbit, but we're wrong, because the rifle shot that shatters the silence didn't get shot for nothing, believe you me, the creature falls midjump, almost dead, legs folding under its spinning body, then curls up and goes still

"Sons alive! didn't miss that'un, did I!"

shouts our Raymond wiping his mustache with the back of his hand

we run toward the hare still twitching with life but not for long, its startled eyes watching us with the submission of the vanquished, of prey sent from this world to the next by our invincible long guns, the animal knows it's dying, it's instinct, man and beast alike know when the end is near, blood gushes from the wound near the hare's head, staining the snow with fresh steaming blood that's clear as water and so red it dims the blinding light piercing our eyes

the rest of us watch as though killing's new to us but the truth is we stopped caring a long time ago, we already know that blood and snow don't mix, we know

then Raymond grabs the hare by the ears and stuffs it into his game bag, he stands up and inspects the fields stretching in every direction

"This way"

he says, sure of himself, sure he's leading us to the right place, where animals go to drink water from the wadi or graze on sparse scrub, but we don't need a leader anymore, the sight of blood has awakened us, and in the time it takes the sun to reach the top of the sky our game bags are filled with hares, rabbits, partridges, and other feathered creatures whose thighs and breasts, nameless or not, will grill just as nicely over our blazing fires

all that meat whets our jaws, gets our mouths salivating with our never-satiated hunger

"Let's go back"

decides Raymond

yes, let's go back and gorge ourselves, let's fill our starving bellies and drink spirits that'll set our insides on fire, let's fuck our moukères whom we'll split open like Christmas hogs

it's almost warm in the sun-dappled snow and we begin to sing loud as we can

Guns firing, never tiring
Pillage and raze, set it ablaze
Choose our prize
This land is ours
to colonize!

as blood drips from our hide bags into the footprints of our soaked mud hooks and vultures spin overhead like tops

as we're crossing the wadi we stumble upon two raggedy Bedouins pissing, bags slung over their shoulders and hoods up, and they don't even have time to hide their balls, we're on 'em so fast, kicking them into the snow, our rifle barrels jammed into their burnooses

"So the little desert rats are showing off their pipes, are they?"

our Raymond snickers to himself and rubs his hands as the Bedouins glare back, sizing him up

"Answer me, goddammit!"

but how can they answer? they don't speak a word of our language, so Raymond gets annoyed, he's a big man, he grabs them by the burnooses and stands them upright

"Nobody pisses in front of Captain Landron's soldiers! no, you kneel and then you thank the brave soldiers who came all the way from France to clean your godforsaken country of its throat-slitting barbarians, and you'd better be near licking the ground as you do!"

the sun's slinking behind the horizon and suddenly the cold bites harder at our faces, it slices deeper into our fingers gripped around our rifles

Raymond shouts himself hoarse for nothing, shaking and punching the two desert rats, who stay quiet, and in the end he decides to bring them to the captain, what else can he do?

"Nothing, Raymond, nothing"

we reply in unison

so we continue on our way, pushing our captives, who are dragging their feet, we're in a hurry to get back to the fonduk and a warm fire, we're tired and cold and can barely see straight, which is exactly why our two rats suddenly barrel through us to try their luck in the field of snow stretching ahead of them

"Lousy whoresons!"

roars our Raymond

he shoulders his rifle and all ten of us follow suit, ten fingers on the trigger, ten shots fired into the evening gloom to bring down the Bedouins, stop them clean in their tracks and make sure this is the last breath they ever take

they fall, and stars of blood on their backs form constellations

we wait to see what will happen, but nothing happens, the snow drinks the men's blood just as it drank the hare's, so we shoulder our rifles again, proper pleased with ourselves, then head back, double quick this time, to the fonduk

behind us the vultures have already spotted the bodies and in silence, in the vast silence heavy with snow falling from the mountains, they dive to whet their beaks.

(HANDS OF TOIL)

And then, since everything in this life must be forgotten or forgiven, we buried our most painful memories in the recesses of our minds, for they are the kind that never fade, and spurred by the inexplicable instinct to survive we resumed our battle against the sun and the barren earth and the Arabs lying in wait day and night for an opportune moment to leap out of the brush and butcher us to bits

as the months passed the vigor the colony lost in the time of cholera returned, our captain doing everything in his power, and he had plenty, to bring us the comforts we were in our rights to demand, a priest came from Algiers to ease our suffering and deliver Mass on Sunday mornings, Father Monin, a jovial bear of a man who didn't mind taking off his cassock to help us build a cob hut with slits for windows in which he improvised an altar and placed rudimentary benches

"My church!"

he exclaimed when the work was done

"Please enjoy, it's open to all"

Rosette, Célestine, and I began to attend Mass every Sunday, there were more followers than could fit inside that sad little church so people would squeeze onto the makeshift pews and oftentimes stand in the dust of a street that wasn't yet a street but would be soon, and together we would pray for our dearly departed and then for our community of survivors that wasn't very hale but dearly needed to be, and our Father Monin, perched on a ladder that served as a pulpit, never missed a chance to needle his flock, for he knew perfectly well that these lambs, women mostly, our skin gray and furrowed from fatigue, our cheeks sunken and our eyes lifeless, had escaped from hell itself, and therefore we were lambs who needed rousing and shaking, to be whipped into shape, so to speak, and comforted in the choice we had made to cross the Mediterranean Sea to colonize lands that would surely, the Republic of France had no doubt about it, make us richer than in our wildest dreams

but could our shattered trust be rebuilt?

as for me, I prayed without conviction, I couldn't help myself, near certain as I was that the words I was saying to God served no purpose, that he didn't hear them, and whenever I listened to Father Monin I would start thinking about something else, like surely his power reached its limits at the gates of hell? and a chuckle would sneak out of my mouth as I watched him wave his hairy paws in the air and then point one confident if not infallible finger above our blanched faces, I would tell myself that I'd have liked to see this man of the cloth at work when the abysses of hell had opened beneath our feet, what would he have done to save Rosette's husband? and my two boys? and Célestine's father and son?

though I always chased those questions from my mind when we emerged from the church at the end of Mass and embraced, blinking under the large African sun, somewhat recomforted, and life was resuming its course, wasn't it? hard to claim otherwise when everything around us was changing, improving, finally taking form

holy Mary mother of God, is your hand in this?

and along with the priest came a schoolteacher who made the trip in the army convoy sent from Bône twice a week to replenish our provisions and equipment, she was a young thing, blonde as wheat, she started teaching our children the very next day in a makeshift shack the captain had the soldiers build out of bamboo and branches from dead trees in the wadi, with a roof of palm leaves as protection from the sun

it's idiotic but we told ourselves, Henri and I, that the school was a sign we were on the right path, that maybe we would succeed if we just worked hard enough on our seven hectares of land

and since each family was allotted one ox from the common stable, one morning we rolled up our sleeves, we set the plow at one end of our two hectares intended for growing wheat and hitched the ox, Henri traced a furrow in ground hardened by years of lying fallow while I held the ox by its harness and led it to the other end of the field

behind me Henri, hands clenched on the plow handles, was pushing like a slave, loaded rifle slung across his back, shirt soon drenched with sweat, and the veins on his brow near popping out of his head from the effort it took to keep the cutting blade from slipping, the earth fighting him at every step as if digging up this cursed land was a sacrilege, but Henri held fast, and when we reached the other end of the field, we stopped to look back and then embraced, shouting

"There's one down!"

it was a good furrow, more or less straight with large pebbly ridges on each side, and we were proud that our hands hadn't forgotten how to till the earth after so many months occupied by the urgency of something else entirely

"Let's go on"

I said, forcing the ox to turn around

we labored till evening beneath a warm autumn sky, pausing only to eat a chunk of bread, take a bite of onion, and drink cool water from our jug, then we returned to the house with the ox and our tools and joined Rosette, who was making soup as she listened to Caroline recite one by one the words her finger was tracing in the reading primer the teacher had given all the students

"Mama, the schoolteacher told us that soon we'll have notebooks, ink, and dip pens"

"She told you that?"

"Yes, she did"

"Then it's going to be a real school, all that'll be left is to build some real walls and put a real roof on top"

Célestine and her son suppered with us, as they did almost every day, they were too alone, too isolated, to get by on their own, and Célestine, keenly aware that it wasn't possible for her to farm her seven hectares, had given her land to us to work, in exchange for which she'd share the harvest, if there was any, and in the meantime she'd accepted the serving job offered her by Gaston Frick, whose tavern was more successful than he could handle

"Well, did you plow the field?"

asked Célestine

"We started"

and I pointed to Henri's red, swollen, and blistered hands

"We've lost the habit, you see, lost the habit entirely, but it'll come back"

we ate soup, drank wine, and said any old thing that popped into our heads with more enthusiasm than we'd had in a long time, long indeed, though Célestine's son, Gérard, didn't talk, ever since his brother was taken by the cholera he'd refused to speak, wouldn't play with the other boys, and glowered at us all as though we each bore some responsibility for the death of his beloved brother

Célestine had taken him to the army doctor, who shrugged and counseled her to have the boy drink herbal tea until his child mind forgot the horrors he'd lived through, and while we were there, I asked the man to examine my daughter too, but he didn't find anything abnormal, Caroline had inexplicably been able to forget the deaths of her two brothers, in appearance at least, concluded the doctor, but then he had the gall to add, be that as it may, madame, a colony's no place for raising children, and hearing that left me speechless, I stormed out without so much as a goodbye, slamming the door behind me

the next day Henri and I returned to our field with the ox following meekly behind, puffing steam out its fly-infested nostrils as though the land to be plowed was so hostile that the poor thing could barely muster its strength, fortunately our two hectares weren't very far from the village, we would be hard at work long before the other settlers who were obliged to walk deep into the brush to reach their fields, often at distances that took them out of eyesight of the soldiers posted on watch around the wall-walk of our new fortified ramparts, which meant we could labor without fear of attack, though Henri insisted on keeping his rifle loaded, but only because he did fear attack, say by a famished

lion or panther, and I can't say he was wrong, seeing the
terrible fate that befell the Marange boy, who had gone
out on his own unarmed to dig a field of potatoes and
gotten himself devoured by one of those desert lions
against which no one stands a chance

holy Mary mother of God, if I had known what was
awaiting us settlers

after the lion ate half of the Marange boy, the men
in the village organized a hunt to catch the beast, which
had long been terrorizing the region, impervious to bullets it would seem, a group of thirty led by the captain
searched the brush for two days but that wicked black-
maned lion avoided every trap, and so as not to return
empty-handed the captain killed a panther that the
men carried back suspended by its legs from a branch
and displayed in the town square

"Henri?"

he was having a rest on a dead tree stump, listening
to the ox chew cud with its eyes closed

"Henri, do you think we'll make it?"

he shrugged

"Have to, don't we"

and looked at me as though he was certain that
whatever awaited us was beyond our strength, all of a
sudden I felt lost, a wisp of straw beneath the vast sky,
abandoned without mercy to the sun, the cholera, and
the shakes, to the wild beasts mad with hunger same
as the natives hostile to our presence who hunted the
outsiders—"roumi"—that we had become to them with

the same ferocity as the lion hunting its prey, because that's what we were becoming—prey

"We've already lost our two boys"

I whispered, my trembling hands hidden in my apron pockets, then took a gulp of air, swelled my chest, and let out a long sigh to exorcise the sense of foreboding squeezing my ribs like a vice

"Let's get on then"

I grabbed the ox's harness, and seeing that, Henri stood, lit his pipe again, closed the cap, and spat in his hands

"Yes, let's"

and we resumed our labor as farmers tearing up earth that since its creation had never, I'm sure of it, felt the blade of a plow, and with each step, despite all our sorrows, I felt a sort of pride and no doubt Henri felt the same, yes, a sort of pride that was perhaps closer to hubris, I don't mind saying it, ill-placed no doubt but justified by the fact that this land long subjected to the whims of the gruesome barbarism that reigned across the African continent for thousands of years was in the end to be drawn into the light by sheer will, by our will, by colonists who, rich or poor, strong or weak, men, women, and children, wanted nothing more than to dig deep, straight furrows in the earth, as we were doing on that autumn afternoon, and harvest wheat, barley, tobacco, and grapes, and countless other riches the land offers when man works it with ardor and intelligence the sun had disappeared behind the mountains as chirping birds emerged from the underbrush and took flight, a red partridge landed on the ridge of a furrow and Henri killed it with one rifle shot that echoed in the farthest reaches of the sky, it was time to stop working

"Henri, shall we visit the cemetery before we go back?"

"If you like"

on the way we met other homebound settlers, they were dragging their feet in the dust but otherwise hiding their fatigue behind the good spirits that set in once the day is finally done, then an ox hitched to a cart balked and blocked the path, and we took the opportunity to exchange pleasantries, and complaints too about the uncultivated land that resisted all our labors

"It's not easy earth, is it"

said someone

then that party headed toward the village as we took the path to the cemetery that had swelled in size from all the dead taken by the cholera and that was growing still because every week someone died of something, I tied the ox to a tree and walked down the row that led to our plot, following Henri, who hadn't waited for me, the dead partridge had bled into the game bag slung over his shoulder and now that bird blood was dripping onto the ground, guiding me better than my memory that often failed me in that maze of wooden crosses

how could it be that so many had died already?

I looked at the family names and given names, the dates of birth and death when there were any, telling myself that these people blindly cut down by Death's scythe had been my companions on the *Labrador*, that we had eaten and slept side by side, emptied our insides together as the frigate pitched on a raging sea, and, when we finally entered the gulf of Bône, cried together in relief

so why were they dead and not me?

when I reached the two crosses planted for my boys I grabbed Henri's arm because every time before I had needed someone's aid to endure the stabbing pain in my heart, a dagger so sharp that my entire body shook, always within an inch of fainting

"Think they're all right?"

I couldn't help saying

"No point asking, when you're in heaven it's always all right"

answered Henri

"I'm not so sure"

then I addressed the question directly to them

"Are you doing all right, my darling boys?"

and waited for their answer in the form of a sign, whatever it was, a butterfly's flittering dance around the crosses, the rustle of dwarf palm leaves, the clatter of a pebble as a lizard crossed the path, this business of signs could take time, Henri patiently waiting beside me, arms crossed, blowing smoke circles into a silence that belonged solely to the dead, the sign could take ages even, but the truth is my question never went unanswered, whether through a butterfly, a palm tree, or a lizard, in the end I always got the answer I needed, Yes, we're doing all right, Mama, you can eat your soup, go to bed, and sleep without a worry till morning

it wasn't much but in those whispers of nature my soothed heart found a way to dress its wounds.

○

The days passed, along with the interminable winter rains, the lion attacks in the night on our cows and sheep, the pillages of our harvests by Arabs from the neighboring douars, the massacres of those settlers who weren't prudent enough

must I speak of things that should never have been?

a couple, a man and woman who had labored to open a makeshift hardware shop, got their wagon mired in the mud on the road to Bône, the convoy continued on ahead, and while the man and woman waited for the help that would be sent back they took shelter under a shady tree, which was when a pack of Arabs from this douar or another leapt out of the brush and slaughtered them

must I speak of things that should never have been?

moukères seething with hatred went after the woman, our neighbor and friend who was six months pregnant, they chopped off her breasts and then slit open her belly and took out her baby, whose barely formed body they left to rot in the sun

holy Mary mother of God, surely it's better to stay my tongue?

the days passed, then the months, and all of it was buried, the interminable rains, the lion attacks, the pillages, and the massacres of some of our number

"I swear to you the culprits will be punished"

promised the captain

and to quiet those who spoke of vengeance and wanted to raze the douars to the ground, he distributed doses of sulfate for us to take every day to fight the deadly malaria fevers

"Rest assured, the government of France, conscious of the troubles that plague you, is looking after your health and your safety!"

but were they truly looking after us from their offices in the palaces of Algiers and ministries of Paris? we weren't so sure, we being the colonists of Algeria, which is undoubtedly why one day the governor of Algeria came to visit us in person, accompanied by General MacMahon and General Canrobert, who, sporting fine military uniforms atop their noble steeds stamping with impatience, congratulated, flattered, and encouraged us, and my they saw far, yes, they saw grand indeed, perched on their horses like pashas, willing to spill as much of their soldiers' blood as was necessary for us all to reap fortune and happiness and then, their cheeks ruddy and bellies full, freshly waxed boots casting gleams of light through the village, they left, because after all the good word needed to be spread elsewhere and everywhere, calm and routine returned to our village, and amid that calm and that routine we didn't forget to take our quinine every morning or set out with rifles loaded to inspect the seeds we had sowed and that were now sprouting, an offering to the sun of thousands of green shoots seeking only to grow and fatten so that we could harvest great baits of wheat, barley, and oat which would be sorely needed when winter set in, no, we didn't forget to resume our daily habits, Mass on Sundays and calls on Sister Catherine, who had settled for good in our village to aid the schoolteacher and doctor and also those settlers stricken by a particularly bad lot, nor did we forget to console our dead who surely felt all alone amid those spindling crosses erected to memorialize names already being erased by the sun and the rain

Henri and I were so busy that we didn't have the slightest notion of what Rosette wanted with us when one night after the fieldwork, as we were giving grass to the rabbits shut in their hutches, my sister planted herself in front of us, hands on her hips, a determined look in her eyes

"I need to talk to you both"

"It is serious?"

"No, it's not serious"

we had our soup as usual with Célestine and her son,
we spoke about spring and what the land might pro-
duce this year if temperatures didn't get too high, if the
sun didn't grind all our efforts to dust, Father Monin
peeked in his head to tell us there was to be a celebra-
tion in the village for Palm Sunday and he'd be needing
some help, we offered him a glass of wine that he drank
quickly before going around to knock on other doors

Célestine said her good nights and left with her boy,
and I went to give a kiss to Caroline, who was already
in her bed, then returned to sit at the table beside my
sister and Henri

"Go on, Rosette, what is it you need to tell us?"

she drank the wine left at the bottom of her glass,
laid her hands flat on the table, and announced

"Here it is, I thought long and hard before making
up my mind but now I'm sure: I want to marry again"

"Marry who?"

asked Henri

"The Gautier fellow, Fernand"

"The one whose parents and wife died from cholera?"

"Yes, that's him"

"What's he been doing since he left the village?"

"He's been farming for a merchant with a large parcel
on the road to Bône, we'll get married and then I'll go to
live with him, I'll mind his two little girls and I'll try to
have a boy"

Henri and I exchanged glances, not knowing what to say

"You think it's too early?"

"No, Rosette, it's not too early, I wouldn't want my sister to sacrifice her life to respect the memory of a man who's no longer here"

Rosette placed her hand on my arm, almost relieved

"I was afraid you and Henri wouldn't agree with my decision"

"You're too young to sacrifice yourself"

the three of us bowed our heads as an evening breeze slipped through the open door, disturbing the hanging lantern and jostling midges onto the table, then a moth resumed its flight around the swinging light, and our faces, which remained in shadow, appeared to deform, grotesquely elongated by the sudden sadness that washed over us, fight it though we did.

○

Rosette and Fernand made a trip to Bône to make it official, and we organized a wedding in our village, it was the first one and had to be a success, we set up trestles and benches in the square, asked Gaston and Célestine to grill meat, cook potatoes, and set aside a few casks of red wine

it was quite the affair, believe me

we spent eight days preparing, eight days because we took care to knock on every door and invite everyone, the folks we knew same as those with whom we hadn't had the chance to become acquainted

and when the big day arrived I woke at dawn and then nudged awake Rosette, who had slept at our house for the last time, and I said to her

"Rosette, it's time"

she looked at me, her eyes full of joy the likes of which I hadn't seen in the village for quite a while, then held out her arms

"Séraphine"

we embraced and kissed, holding tight to one another with tears in our eyes, the light of a day we wouldn't soon forget was trickling inside along with the birds' sharp trilling and roosters' bossy crowing and the distant intermingled sound of hooves stamping and wooden clogs clicking as men led their animals to the fields

as Caroline slept, and with Henri already gone to work our plot, we rushed to the safety of the garden hut, poured large buckets of water over our naked bodies and washed ourselves from head to toe until our skin was red and shiny and had regained some of its former glow

Rosette and Fernand didn't have to be at the church until late afternoon, once the fieldwork was finished, so I had the whole day to prepare the bride, who had tried on her white dress ordered in Bône ten times, a simple gown that didn't have much lace or much of a train but that was a true wedding dress all the same, it had to be taken in a little at the waist and around the neckline which revealed too much of my sister's breasts, she'd always had a generous bosom

busy hands and not a minute to waste

but come six o'clock Rosette was ready and Fernand, who had arrived at the village in a cart drawn by a handsome horse, was shuffling around in the garden with Henri, returned from the fields

ladies from the neighboring houses tied ribbons and flowers to the handles of the cart and placed chairs in its bed, then we took our places, Caroline in a flowery dress that Sister Catherine had found for her, me in the blue gown from France that I'd never had the occasion to wear, and Rosette between us, reigning like an Algerian queen under the evening sky, hair curled with an iron, mouth painted red, a bouquet of forget-me-nots in one hand, the other waving to folks who came to their doorsteps to see her

the driver made the round of the village as we'd asked, and how proud the three of us were to be paraded before our neighbors' homes so nicely coiffed and dressed, trailed by the sounds of children shouting merrily and dogs barking as the large evening birds, heads tilted to watch us pass, offered their commentary from the rooftops

when the driver stopped the horse in front of the church, there were already lots of people waiting for us, Father Monin in his old gold-embroidered chasuble, boasting a broad smile that split his face from cheek to cheek, the captain, the doctor, and the schoolmistress beside Sister Catherine, and many more, all with that same smile, and we smiled back, then Henri and Fernand came over to the cart and lifted us down by our waists, setting us on the rug before the church door

"Go on in, please"

said Father Monin and in silence we walked to the altar draped in a white sheet and decorated with two bouquets of brightly colored flowers, palm leaves hung from the ceiling formed a canopy buzzing with flies and bees, and Rosette and Fernand sat on the two chairs presiding before the altar while the men and women of the village, the women mainly, squeezed onto the pews, and those who couldn't find a place to sit waited outside in the softened light of that spring evening

Father Monin didn't keep us long, he led us in singing the customary psalm that asks the faithful to trust in the Lord, then invited the bride and groom to exchange their consent and finally he blessed the rings Fernand had brought, fine gold rings worn by his mother and father before they died from cholera, and concluded the ceremony by delivering the nuptial blessing

> *O Heavenly Father*
> *Graciously crown Rosette with your blessing*
> *so she may fulfill her calling of good wife and mother,*
> *and bring warmth to her home with a love*
> *that is pure and tender.*
> *Bestow your blessing also, O Lord, on Fernand,*

*So that he may be a faithful and devoted husband
and attentive father.*

husband and wife kissed, and the small bronze
church bell, which the priest had ordered from Bône,
blessed, and placed on a tall wooden three-legged stool
flush against the wall, and that for one month been un-
failingly announcing the start and end of Mass, now
that bell rang at full peal to make it known throughout
the village, along every trail in the wilderness, to the
very bottom of the wadis, and all the way to the Arab
douars that my beloved sister Rosette had married in a
second nuptial Fernand Gautier

my sister emerged from the church on her new husband's arm, Célestine tossed a handful of rice at them,
our nearest neighbors followed suit, there were cries
of joy and laughter as crisp as an apple, people rushed
to greet the newlyweds, the captain shook Fernand's
hand, kissed the bride, and gave a short speech to which
Rosette and Fernand listened as they tried to keep a
straight face, the evening light lingering on their foreheads with such tenderness that you'd have thought
God himself was trying to make an appearance

and this happiness that fell upon us out of the blue
scared me, I felt a sudden shiver down my spine and my
feet fail me

but it lasted only a split second, just long enough for
me to grab my husband's hand, an instant later the feeling was gone, Rosette held out her perfumed arms and

for the second time that day we embraced tightly as two sisters who had always loved each other

after the ceremony

after the manifold congratulations, the sky lit up with a thousand obliging stars, and the square with a thousand lanterns and lamps, and the whole farming colony, men, women, and children, sat down at the tables to eat grilled meat, chops, hocks, livers, kidneys, pounds of tripe, and pounds of sausage served to enthusiastic roars by Gaston and his helpers on wooden boards gleaming with grease

"Three cheers for the newlyweds!"

and the men harried from working the earth served themselves wine in whatever receptacles they could find, glasses, bowls, metal goblets, porringers, and drank themselves dizzy on French piquette that descended into their chests like a cure-all fire

we had collectively decided to claim this nuptial night as our own and to think of nothing but eating, drinking, and merrymaking, driven to excess by a force that had reawakened in each of us and was bringing us back to life in all its sound and fury

"Three cheers for the newlyweds!"

thrilled to be alive and to be making it known, we raised our glasses, bowls, and goblets in a salute

"Three cheers for the newlyweds!"

to the sky and its stars, to the moon that had come out for the occasion, its benevolent head tilted over us,

to the ill-tempered African soil that was getting its just
deserts

everything that could be eaten was eaten, meat,
potatoes, garden vegetables, oranges and lemons from
Bône and Algiers, baskets of almonds and dates, and a
wedding cake, a shortbread concoction garnished with
cream upon which Gaston had stuck a marzipan heart,
bellies were full and bursting with gas, cheeks crimson,
eyes shining with mischief, shirt collars began to open,
corsets to unfasten, belts loosened a few notches, why
hold back? and the grease and wine dribbling down
men's chins had an odd effect, they set to burping, fart-
ing, and spitting, all their primal desires roused, why
hold back? it was time to enjoy what had been given us
and so we did

the accordion player took out his instrument and
climbed onto a table with a violinist he'd found in another village, they started playing French tunes we all
still remembered, our heads were spinning and our bodies pitching like boats on angry seas, we no longer knew
where we were, we looked up at the sky, we looked at the
miserable wooden cabins that served as our homes, at
the cloud of flies swirling around the bones abandoned
on the tables, at Rosette and Fernand, who were dancing as though they were at a ball back home

where were we?

women struggling to stay upright dragged men pick-
led on grease and wine onto the dance floor, I grabbed

Henri by the hand and forced him to take me in his arms and lead me in the waltzes and polkas that I had loved when I was a young girl and didn't yet know what life had in store for me

and even when Rosette and Fernand snuck away I kept dancing, accepting invitations from married and unmarried men alike, taking the arm offered by Gaston, then the camp doctor, and even the captain who waltzed with me for a long time, hands firmly around my waist and pressing his military body against mine

where did we go?

and we kept drinking the wine Gaston served us, as our tuckered children fell asleep on the tables, and we kept eating what was left of the meat and cake in the dying light of the lanterns that went out one after the next

and we kept dancing and dancing and dancing

and at the first glimmers of dawn the accordion player and the violinist dead on their feet stopped playing, there were no more men to waltz the women, they were snoring underneath the tables and against the walls, sitting in the dust, lush off wine they wouldn't forget anytime soon, I found Célestine and sat beside her on the bench where Caroline was sleeping and as I put my espadrilles back on I asked her

"Tell me, Célestine, I'm dying to know the name of that curly-haired fellow you were dancing with all night"

"Joseph, he's a friend of Fernand, he lives in Bône"

"And what does he do?"

"He's a shoemaker"

her fingers were absent-mindedly pressing into the meat of her thighs

"You going to see him again?"

"I think so, it's nearing time I got remarried too"

she darted a look at me and when she saw I was smiling, she smiled back

Henri joined us after paying the two musicians and seeing all that had been left on the ground and the tables, he said

"Let's sleep first, we'll clean the square later"

Célestine and I both nodded in agreement, Henri picked up Caroline, took a last glance at the clutter of tables covered with stains and scraps, then we went home, shooing away the dogs dashing between our legs to squabble over bones

"Where's your boy?"

asked Henri

"He went home to bed"

"Didn't he have fun?"

Célestine looked up and with a sigh studied the sky whose stars and moon were beginning to fade, as if she was searching those vast celestial bodies for an answer to his question, and not finding one she said

"I don't know."

(BLOODBATH)

We fattened up, sprouted paunches and double chins

and the day we leave the fonduk, Captain Landron, same as us soldiers, looks as if he's been stuffed to the gills, gorged on the blood of the animals hunted every day and tender, perfumed moukère flesh

he assembles everyone in the light-drenched court-yard, his soldiers, his harem, the rest of the pigheaded Arabs, the old men and women with crooked spines and the urchins lousy with lice, and our captain is mighty proud to show off his lion's mane, a magnificent mop of curls that he hasn't cut in three months that now hides his forehead and ears and flows down his meaty neck, a grandiose crown atop a face so bloated that his two large bloodshot eyes are drowning in it

"We'll be back"

he thunders

"We'll be back, that's for sure, so be ready, sand rats, keep your moukères nice and warm for next year! Christ almighty, I'll miss those females!"

he goes to mount his horse but has so much trouble that he needs a hand, a good heave-ho to the rear, all the exertion leaves him near-bursting at the seams, blubber overheated and panting like a nag, the blood rises so quick to his face that our captain looks as if he's about to explode but once he's confidently in the saddle, boots fixed in the stirrups, his pride is immediately restored, then, chest thrust forward, voice as commanding as ever, he demands to be brought his gandoura, which has been washed ten times in mountain water so its whiteness will impose respect from the desert vermin he's pacifying, he drapes the tunic over his shoulders and lets the ends fall onto the horse's rump, then spurs the animal, which rises on its hind legs with a neigh

it's such a beautiful sight that we feel shivers run down our leathery skin, because if the land and the sky belong to our captain, and they do, by the power of his conquering sword I maintain that they do, then this land and this sky belong to us warriors too

the horse falls back onto all fours as the women in the captain's harem weep his departure, spilling tears on the animal's hooves and the leather of his army boots

"Onward, soldiers"

at his order, which he addresses to the bright light filling the sky, our column assembles and without a glance at the moricauds who served us so well, we march like kings through the fonduk archway and into the dust and sun that's returned to warm our hides

"Did you load your rifles, soldiers?"

"Yes, captain"

"And sharpen your bayonets?"

"Yes, captain"

our swinish voices vibrate like drums, sending lizards scattering and crows into flight

"Then get ready, soldiers, because where we're headed, there's a revolt brewing, the natives don't want to pay the taxes they owe France, but they'll pay them whether they like it or not, otherwise it's the razzia, you hear me, soldiers?"

"We hear you, captain!"

he shakes his mane and stands in his stirrups, searching the hill's deceptive curves for signs of revolt

"And do you know what that means, soldiers?"

"We know, captain!"

"It means that we'll show no mercy, dammit! it means we won't blink at running through the rebels one by one, then burning down their homes and razing their crops, all in the name of the law, of our fair right as colonizers who came here to pacify lands too long abandoned to barbarism, do you understand, soldiers?"

"We do, captain!"

"I hope so"

he wipes his mouth and then takes a sip of water

"I hope so because this fire'll need stoking in the days to come, I said it once and I'll say it again, we're

off to quell a revolt, and if you lot want to turn back
into the raging bulls you used to be, if you want to leave
behind a trail of blood and bones, it's important, what
am I saying?! it's vital that you lose some weight, that
you unearth the muscles buried under those three-
month-old blankets of fat until the whole pack of you
are skinny enough to fuck a sand mosquito, just take a
look at yourselves! am I right?"

"Yes, captain, you're right!"

"So sweat it off, goddammit, sweat off those rolls of
fat from sunrise to sunset, and remember, I've got my
eye on you, my little piggies, I want to see your coats
and trousers drenched in sweat, I want to see steam
coming off your spines, and too bad about the smell,
you bastards, too bad if it stinks to high heaven, I don't
care if it gets riper than a month-old mango in here,
if the stink of you attracts entire colonies of enraged
hornets"

our captain talks our ears off beneath a sweltering
sun until nightfall, until the sun sinking behind the
horizon shuts him up, and in the silence at last granted
to us we have to walk no less than one league before he
lifts one arm

"Halt!"

and points out some acacias near a marabout in ruin

"That's where we'll bivouac, my brave men, we've
walked enough for today, don't you think?"

"Yes, captain, we're played out"

and in the next instant we drop our gear and plant our rifles in the sand, we toss off our coats and shakos as we cast side glances at the menacing darkness, it's time to light some fires and quickly, at the captain's order four of the men leave to fetch wood, they return with armfuls that are piled on the three fires that have been lit by then, then they set off again with more arms in tow because we need bigger logs, they go all the way to the wadi bed, cutting up trees uprooted by the spring floods

soon enough our fires are crackling, roaring like ten thousand forges, the flames blazing blue in the sky before they cool and fade in the cloying vastitudes of a dusk that bears us no good will, that's for sure, but at least we know that the fires kindled through the night will keep at bay the desert lions and yataghan-wielding barbarians salivating to slit our hides

as our two cooks bustle around their mess kits preparing supper, we pull out our pipes and light some tobacco all the while searching for a spot to rest our backsides, then we hear Raymond say

"Captain, something's wrong...Rouzec didn't come back from firewood duty"

"What are you on about, Bourdin?"

"We looked for him, captain, but we can't find him, he's gone"

"Keep looking!"

so we all look, we retrace our steps, we go in circles, we search by the light that is already fading and full of deceptive shadows, but we find nothing, nothing but emptiness and silence

"No sign of him, he's disappeared"

"Christ alive!"

yells our captain, he asks for help mounting his horse and saber in hand spurs his steed and takes off at full tilt in the direction of the wadi

we watch him bayonet the dying twilight, he's fit to be tied and when Captain Landron is fit to be tied it's best to keep your distance from his blade, eventually the horse disappears into the river valley and as we have nothing to do but wait for our captain's return we decide it's wisest to pick up our rifles and patrol the camp

it's almost pitch-black when we hear hooves at last but is it our captain's horse? we can't tell until it comes closer, and then the firelight reveals that it is in fact our captain's steed and that its rider is in no laughing mood, not in the slightest, his jaws soldered tight enough to break bone, eyes dancing a jig in the light of the flames, in shock, surely, from what they saw, and his crimson cheeks twitching with every step

"Those bastards!"

he roars

"Those shifty godforsaken savages!"

he spits fuming gobs of phlegm, looks around for an enemy to carve into bits, and not finding one his saber lands in the fire, where it quivers with rage amid the flying embers

"They beheaded the man! shortened our Rouzec a good foot with their yataghans, and the most barbaric part is that the sons-of-dogs took his head with them, but for what? I ask you, for what? Christ alive!"

we offer to help him dismount but our captain isn't hearing it, he wants to stay in the saddle, master of his troops and the roaring fires and the night itself that has finally blanketed our camp in darkness, because he needs a place of elevation from which to unleash his anger, a strategic position to ensure his declaration of war will echo in every corner of the sky

"They better not think they intimidate me! I ask you, men, has anyone ever intimidated Captain Landron?"

"Of course not, captain!"

we respond in chorus

"So a few moricauds armed with rusty pistols and yataghans won't be the first, not by a long shot! I'm going to take good care of those decapitating barbarians, oh yes, I'll chop them into little pieces and make myself a hearty African stew! they think they scare me? ha! they think they're our match? ha! they'll see how a man like Captain Landron takes his revenge, and they'll remember it for the rest of their days, if they have any left that is, because no one will be spared, every last one of those Christian-mangling bastards will bleed like a pig, old, young, couscous-fattened moukères and their sniveling desert urchins, crippled, hunchbacked, bald, mangy, fat, skinny, one-legged, one-eyed, I don't give a damn! and no later than tomorrow morning, I tell you now, soldiers! it's time to polish your rifles and sharpen your bayonets because at daybreak I want you ready to march, will you be ready, men?"

"We'll be ready, captain!"

he nods, looks at us as a father would his sons, proud to recognize himself in each of us, and that recognition settles his nerves

"Ten of you go get Rouzec, he's in the wadi behind the big white rock, take torches and be careful"

we bury Valentin Rouzec's body beneath an acacia tree, rolled in a sheet of canvas so we can forget he's missing his head, and Lepéreux sticks a cross in the godforsaken Algerian earth

then we gather around the fires and eat the potato stew the cooks prepared for us.

○

We're a sight to see, soldiers marching in step, four by four, in the gray light of the dawning day and a silence so deathly it frightens the sun cowering behind the mountains

a sight to see

faces long as a month of Sundays, puffing like galley slaves and wrung out like old hags after our hard night in the devil's darkness

a sight to see

wrapped in his gandoura our captain is ruminating his revenge, he doesn't see or hear anyone, no, he's

already on maneuvers, sending his bloodthirsty warriors to storm the sleeping village, leaving our foes no
time to reach for a pistol or a yataghan, he's drooling
at the thought, ass twitching with impatience in the
saddle

suddenly he spits out the chewed-up remnants of his
cigar and stands up in his spurs to point at a row of
lime-washed gourbis at the bottom of an embankment

"We have them, men!"

he shouts as he turns back to us

"We'll show them what it costs to behead a French
soldier!"

and we hurtle down the embankment to surround
the village, ignoring the donkeys in their pens, the
turtledoves cooing, the smells of piss, vermin, and
dead rat lashing our nostrils

we freeze, muscles tensed, eyes wild, ears buzzing,
we all try to catch our breaths to no avail, it's time, captain, give the order, liberate us, release us so we can
rush our foes and pig-stick them the way they deserve

and the order comes

"Charge!"

a terrible howl of rage rises from our collective chest,
it swells and overflows, it rattles the walls that abruptly
begin to shake, it swallows all the light in the sky

we smash down doors and the men who start awake
and attempt to block our path get a bayonet in the belly,
they leak like goatskins, Arabs on a spit, but we keep

stabbing and slicing as their womenfolk scream and spin, banging into the walls like trapped flies, arms waving and feet stamping as they smother their terrified children's sobs in their rags

"No mercy, soldiers!"

screams the captain

"Avenge Rouzec!"

his saber, already crimson with the blood of the men and women he slaughters, inspires us

"Avenge Rouzec, my brave men!"

invigorates us

"Avenge him!"

ignites us

his all-mighty saber is the scourge of God, the weapon of his justice, and our duty as soldiers is to obey him, to spill the bad blood of any who oppose his might

and we are avenging him, captain, rage seeping from our brandy-gorged guts, we carve up that evil flesh without tiring, are you watching, captain? soon we'll be wading through pools of blood that spread like a curse, pools that join to form boiling rivers, are you proud of us, captain? boiling rivers of bad blood that flow over thresholds and mingle with rubbish in the alleys infested with dung flies

yes, we know you're proud of us, captain

and when we walk out the smashed doors in search of fresh air and sun, when the silence falls onto our steaming shoulders as our hearts clatter in chests drenched in enemy blood, well now we feel the urge to pull out our pipes and stuff them to the brim and inhale enough tobacco to detonate a man's brain, moments like this are worth more than all the gold in this cursed world, and the boys who don't smoke get to calmly slitting the donkeys' throats and any other throats they can get their hands on, a ewe, some hens, a lame dog that doesn't have time to run

the captain astride his horse leaves us to make the rounds of the village now emptied of its inhabitants, he's talking to himself, addressing the mountains, the murderous heathens he thinks are hiding among the rocks, or maybe the crows already ominously whirling above the gourbis, he repeats that his saber will spare no one, that he has the god of the Christians with him and that the Christian god is not in the habit of forgiving anything to those who have wronged him

"Christ alive, when will you stubborn sand devils understand?"

his booming voice echoes in the silence like a voice from heaven

"France has been given the divine mission to pacify your barbaric lands and offer your empty brainboxes the splendors of a millennia-old culture, whether you like it or not! any who refuse our outstretched hands will be plowed down, crushed to dust, sliced into tiny pieces by the steel of our sabers and bayonets!"

he roars and thunders like a troop of cavalry but not one of those dogs shows himself to wave the white flag, captain can wait long as he likes in his seven-league boots and his pasha's gandoura, what he's waiting for will never come, no question about it if you ask us soldiers who've worn out our mud hooks trampling every damn road in this Arab hell swamp

we exchange glances, suckling our pipes like a Dutch girl's teats, and we're all thinking that our dear captain better not lose his mind one of these days, no sir, better not, because if he did lose his mind in the middle of this wasteland of sand and rock, what would become of the rest of us?

he circles around the village three more times, gandoura flapping in the wind, blazing mane caught in the net cast by the setting sun, and saber pointed he threatens the sky once again, he swears to split this cursed African land down the middle, disembowel its mountains, and dry up every wadi and well

then he stops his horse white with foam and shouts

"Burn it all to the ground! pillage and plunder, soldiers! take whatever you can"

and by the end of his sentence we've stuffed our pipes in our pockets and begun our raid, no, gold rush, a satanic mesmerizing rush that makes our mouths salivate and our pissers harden in our trousers, Christ alive, Christ alive, with ferocious hands we eviscerate bags and trunks, roll up rugs, rip necklaces from moukères' bloody necks, cut off any finger with a bauble, ears too, male or female, that believe me are worth their weight in gold on the black market in Algiers

Christ alive, Christ alive!

next a group of us set the gourbis ablaze while the others take their axes to the groves of olive, almond, and apricot trees, which get thrown into the flames consuming the village

two thick columns of smoke rise in the sky dancing a somber jig, and a fire like that can be seen from so many miles away, a fire like that promises such horrors that the sons of Mahomed must be pissing in their burnooses

no, we're no angels.

○

For two days without end, we pillage and burn the villages that have the misfortune of finding themselves in our path, our eyes stinging from the flames and ears sore from the piercing screams and nostrils rankled by the smell of blood and guts in the air we breathe in day and night

"Aren't we done yet, captain?"

"Not yet, goddammit! not yet!"

he responds, one flinty eye scanning the horizon

but on the third day all we find are villages emptied of their inhabitants, no more rebels, no more moukères, no more snot-nosed kids, and not a single animal to slaughter and fill our bellies

"Now where could our cussed moricauds be?! where are those raggedy lily-livered rats hiding?"

and in the middle of one village the captain's nag starts to buck and kick, rageful sparks flying from its hooves, the horse is as hopping mad as its master, and like its master it's hungry for some Berber meat, the animal enjoys trudging through blood and snapping at moukère rears, makes a nice change from all that marching in a line squashed between the captain's thighs

Lepéreux points to movement high on the mountain

"Look, captain, there they are"

the captain turns around, one hand cupped over his forehead to block the sun, and blinks

"What the hell are they doing in those rocks?"

"The mountain has deep caves, captain, they're hiding there until we leave"

anger mounts immediately, his crimson face darkens to purple, he begins to sweat from the sun beating down on us, his face is dripping, his chest boiling, thighs steaming, then he flings his immaculate gandoura at his aide-de-camp

"Do you reckon, soldiers, that we're going to take this lying down?"

"No, captain, we don't"

"Quite right! Christ alive, of course we're not!"

he mops his forehead with the back of his sleeve

"Because I'm going to teach those bloodthirsty ruffians the meaning of obedience, I'm going to show them what it costs to play rebel, to not pay the taxes they owe France and to make a collection of our poor soldiers' heads, hellfire! who do they think they are?!"

his eyes search the mountainside and the tip of his saber casts lightning at the runaways

"What are you thinking in your pig-shit for brains? that France is going to make an exception just for you? when meanwhile these pacification campaigns are running the government coffers dry, since it's gonna take tens of thousands of soldiers, what am I saying? hundreds of thousands of soldiers to hammer the reason for our presence on your godforsaken devil lands into your pigheaded pig-shit brains! I've said it before and I'll say it again, all we want is to raise you to our level, to bring you into our world that any way you look at it is better than yours!"

bitter saliva catches in his throat, obliging him to spit on the ground so he can finish

"And to all who have resisted, are resisting, and will resist the enlightenment we're bringing them, hear me well when I say you can be sure, Christ alive! that you will be exterminated and not the slightest ounce of pity will stay our sabers, rifles, and bayonets! if we have to exterminate you one by one from the shores of the Mediterranean to the farthest reaches of the Sahara, well then we will!"

our captain stops talking, he said what he had to say and he's proud of his speech, same way we're proud to have a leader who can give such a speech, his voice echoes in the distance, bouncing again and again off the surrounding rocks until finally silence creeps back, it grabs us by the throat and slides like an eel into our ears as vultures leisurely circle over the abandoned village, their wings casting shadows onto our backs wet with sweat

then, amid the silence, a shot fired from the mountain tells us what we have to do

"Charge, men!"

screams our captain, beside himself

"No quarter!"

in shirtsleeves and even bare-chested, we run full steam toward the caves, unburdened of our kits, coats, and shakos, we're faster than greased lightning, little mind the bullets buzzing past our ears, soon enough we take the positions those sand devils thought they could hold, we skewer four or five them with our bayonets and we gather at the entrance to two caves in which the whole village tribe has taken refuge

our captain catches up gasping for breath

"What do we do, captain?"

"We do nothing, goddammit! what can we possibly do? the cave neck is too narrow to attack and these moricauds know it! they know that if we force our way in we'll get a hail of iron right in the kisser, maybe that's exactly what they were planning, but I swear to you, we won't fall into their trap!"

he paces before the caves, swivels back and forth, stabs the myrtle bushes with his saber, kicks pebbles hurtling down the slope and dragging others with, he puts his captain's mind to work, racks his brainpan to find a way to cut the enemy down to size, because he doesn't want to lose face, certainly not! for how could a captain in the French army lose face in front of a few dozen moricauds? he can't, period, he simply can't, so he needs those cussed hell devils stone-dead and so do we, we need them skinned and gutted and on their way to Allah's seven heavens

suddenly the captain's eyes light up with a devilish gleam

"I've got it, men! I found the trick we'll play on our poor little Bedouins! and it will be quite the lesson for all the gourbis in these parts, believe me"

proud of the scheme he's concocted, he gathers us round and gives his orders

"We're going to smoke them out!"

"Smoke them out, captain?"

"Yes, smoke them out, set fire at the cave entrances and let the fumes do our job for us"

to flee the soldiers' unrivaled cruelty, the entire village, men and women, children and the elderly, carrying their jewels, rugs, precious teapots, and provisions of tea, wheat, and dried fruit, with their sheep, donkeys, and faithful dogs in tow, rose well before dawn to take refuge in the deep caves that had saved their lives many a time but that, on this day, to their great misfortune, would aid them no more

again with the commentary?!

and per the captain's orders that's what we did, two roaring fires were lit and fed through the night as screams, sobs, and prayers did their best to cross the flames barring the entrances *trapped deep within the caves by suffocating smoke, they fall one by one, their tortured lungs desperately seeking a respite from this hell*

enough already! can the remarks and leave us in peace!

how many die in this gruesome manner? how many will have as their only resting ground these caves that long served as dens for desert lions?

enough, goddammit! war is war!

though the wails coming from the cave mouths do fray our nerves, they make us want to cut out our enemies' tongues, how come they didn't learn to die in silence like the rest of us?

it's true, we're no angels

the endless wails go on until sunset, until not a soul is left alive inside those cursed caves, then we stop stoking the fires, we let them burn out and in the falling night we climb down the mountain to make our quarters in the gourbis forever emptied of their inhabitants

no, we're no angels.

(HANDS OF TOIL)

Did you think our troubles had ended?

don't know much about cruelty if you believe it can be exhausted by man, whether he's the governor of Algeria, general of the armed forces, or the holy messenger himself

despite the quinine sulfate, which had to be paid for at present and not for cheap, with plenty among us without the means to buy it, there were deaths every week, people succumbing to brain fevers and diarrhea and all manner of insidious disease, with those who survived looking as if they'd been through hellfire, their cheeks splotched red and the skin around their mouths cracking with scabs, their eyes yellow from Lord knows what internal ailment

and all the while the captain kept saying that we shouldn't lose hope, that we were on the right path, on our rightful God-given path

"My dear compatriots, after working side by side with you day and night, it's clear to me who I am dealing with, and I am compelled to applaud your labor, courage, and patience, for, from colony to colony, I see how you dig your hands deep into this ungrateful earth and yank it from the darkness in which it's been languishing for more centuries than I can count, I see how you bring it into the light and plant your seeds, and is there a more noble task? I ask you, my compatriots, is there a more noble task? believe me when I say that each and every one of you, man, woman, or child, belongs to the race of the just, by which I mean the race of man that carries in its bosom the generous sons of progress, the pioneers, trailblazers, and builders already distinguishing themselves and who will soon shine across the entirety of the Algerian territory"

lying on our straw pallets, we weighed both sides of the captain's impassioned speeches, but as for me, a woman whose remaining strength was dwindling with each passing day, brought to my knees before my two sons' graves, I couldn't forget what it had already cost me to play colonist on behalf of the glorious Republic of France, and on some nights tears of sadness streamed down my cheeks, and on others, tears of rage

and then to add to our woes one day the captain gathered us in the square to tell us that tribes from the nearby douars had revolted, roused by their marabouts, and slaughtered laborers, burned countless harvests, and threatened agricultural colonies

"There are hundreds of them"

he repeated

hundreds galloping through these parts, screaming like banshees on their Arab steeds, brandishing their yataghans and rifles before the ramparts of terrorized villages

"They could be here by tomorrow"

we settlers flew into a panic, there were things to be done and as quickly as possible, gather the animals from the fields and bring them into the safety of the barns, close and fortify the two gates to the village, and the thirty soldiers under the captain's orders went to stand guard on the ramparts, rifles loaded and eyes peeled

I slept poorly that night, ears pricked for any sounds, my heart racing at the slightest crack or creak, a bird pitter-pattering on the roof, a dog barking, and I couldn't help but think about my sister and her husband isolated on their farm with not a soul to count on if by misfortune the insurgents attacked them, Fernand's hunting rifle certainly wouldn't scare those raging devils so what would become of them? I tossed and turned in my bed not daring to answer my own question for so long that when dawn showed its face I rose, dressed, and not daring to wake Henri I went outside and ran to the ramparts, I climbed the ladder that led to the sentry walk, where I found the soldiers standing guard but also other settlers who, like me, hadn't been able to sleep

"Well?"

"Well nothing"

replied one soldier

everything was calm, the horizon empty but for two dogs wandering the path to the cemetery and crows pecking for worms in Tavernier's plowed field

"Shouldn't trust what you see"

said Mémé Ferrand, a loudmouth who wasn't scared of anyone or anything, and who was respected by all the settlers because she was said to have killed two Arab mule thieves with her own hands

"Why not?"

I asked

"Because it's precisely when we don't see 'em and don't hear 'em that the enemy is the most dangerous, what's not to say they're hiding behind those hills, waiting for the right moment to strike?"

Mémé Ferrand wasn't wrong, the sun hadn't even reached the rooftops when over a hundred men on horseback appeared at the top of a ridge and hurtled down screaming as they waved their weapons in the air to show us their rage and their thirst to slit every one of our throats

a bugle sounded to warn the village and all the men came running rifles in hand as the captain shouted at the women and children to stay in their homes, I crossed paths with Henri on his way to join the other men on the ramparts

"Célestine and her boy are hiding in our house, Caroline was too frightened to get out of bed, hurry back to her"

"Henri?"

I caught hold of his sleeve and he looked at me as though he had already understood what I was about to say

"Don't get yourself killed"

he nodded and muttered something that I couldn't make out, then he took off running as the sound of the insurgents' fanatical screams drew closer

all day long the Arabs galloped around the ramparts, firing rifle shots that often missed their target but all the same wounded three settlers and one soldier, who were immediately taken to Gaston's tavern-cum-infirmary, where the doctor, Sister Catherine, and the schoolmistress removed the bullets and then cleaned and bandaged the wounds, while also calming the women who arrived in a frantic state at the tavern door in need of reassurance while they awaited the captain's report

at nightfall the riders stopped harrying us, they lit fires and prepared to spend the night not far beyond our walls

in the church square where men and women alike had gathered, the captain addressed the colony, taking stock of an exhausting day during which our soldiers had had to repel the assailants attempting by any means to breach our defenses, but we had only four wounded whereas our rifles had killed at least ten Arabs, that was a good tally, and the captain thanked us for having fought so well though he was careful not to claim victory all the same, for he knew that our resistance had its limits, that there weren't enough of us to withstand the insurgents' assault for long

"Today there were a hundred of them, but tomorrow they might be three hundred or a thousand storming our village"

I brought my hand to my chest, as did most of the women, the gesture instinctive for those of us who could easily imagine our fate if those barbarians got their hands on us, heavy silence fell like lead on our shoulders, leaving our mouths dry as cotton, almost unable to breathe, until finally someone asked

"Well what can we do?"

the captain straightened up and this time he had a gleam in his eye

"At midnight I'll send a soldier on our best horse to Bône to warn the commander and tomorrow night at the latest a squadron will be here to grind those fanatics to dust"

and when it was dark enough, the Bizot boy, who had volunteered, mounted the horse the captain had selected and took advantage of the welcome obscurity to slip through the enemy lines and gallop at full pelt to Bône

the night was short, Célestine and I put our children
to bed and prepared food and drink for the men guard-
ing the ramparts while Henri patrolled the streets with
two neighbors, all bearing rifles, surveying the houses
and barns until dawn, but not a noise or shadow to
report

life had come to a halt, outside the houses and within,
and the silence that had taken its place was troubling,
we wondered why had the crickets stopped chirping
and the birds stopped pattering on the roofs, why had
the dogs stopped barking, were these bad omens? Célestine and I were sure they were, so sure that neither
of us, though we were so tired we could barely stand or
see straight, was able to fall asleep

and the next morning before the sun had even risen
the cavalcade resumed around the ramparts, the insurgents more rageful than before, they roared like lions
and cackled like hyenas as shots fired out, there weren't
a thousand of them circling the village but a lot more
than the previous day, three hundred maybe, and we
women started to think that if reinforcements didn't
arrive very soon we were all going to be killed

twice Henri popped into the house, flushed with ex-
citement, dust in his hair, eyes bulging, hands covered
in blood

"Something to drink, quick! I'm parched"

I rushed over with the pitcher

"Are you hurt?"

"No, it's Bidault, he took some buckshot to the gut"

"Is he dead?"

"They carried him to the infirmary"

he drank the whole pitcher of water and raced back to the first village gate, which the Arabs were trying to break down

I doubt we would have lasted another hour if the squadron's bugle hadn't rung out in the distance, we all rushed onto the sentry walk and watched as rows of spahis in red tunics emerged from the fog of heat and at their captain's order charged the war-crazed Arabs who had been besieging us since the previous day, with sabers whirling, our soldiers massacred our foes, stabbing chests and lopping off heads and slicing off hands that had already done us too much harm, and quick enough the survivors fled, chased away by the captain and his troops' vengeful blades

we immediately reopened the village gates, crying aloud our joy to still be alive as breathless soldiers on horses sticky with foam passed through, we served cool wine to the men and to the horses, water and oats, the captains greeted each other, then the squadron left for other villages also under threat

that night we buried the Arabs' mutilated bodies in a common grave for fear that the bloody flesh would attract the lions and panthers always on the hunt, and in the days that followed we fortified the sections of the rampart that had been damaged by our assailants and resumed our labors in the rampaged fields

"Do you think we'll ever live in peace?"

I was seated on a rock, watching a vulture fly in circles overhead, I didn't dare tell Henri how tired I felt

"It's over, Séraphine, the insurgents went back to their gourbis, and the most ferocious ones were killed"

"I haven't heard from my sister"

"You're bound to soon"

replied Henri, still hacking at the roots of a dwarf palm

"I'm not so sure"

"Why do you say that?"

"I have a bad feeling"

and I was right to worry because two days later the convoy from Bône brought us bad news indeed, a merchant recounted in great detail the destruction wreaked by insurgents in the more remote zones, how they burned crops and set houses afire and massacred entire families of settlers in the most gruesome of ways

"The Cyprien, Gautier, Pigeon, Dagas, and Aubrey farms all went up in flames, and I can tell you those yataghan-waving fanatics didn't spare a soul"

"Did you say Gautier?"

I was hoping I'd heard wrong

"Yes, the Gautier farm, with the two big dovecotes"

Henri was beside me, I grabbed his arm for support and said to him

"Come, let's go home"

I thought I had enough strength to reach the house but I was wrong, halfway there my sight began to blur, the light of that baleful summer night dimmed, I paused, trying to calm my racing heart and catch my breath, to no avail, all of a sudden, my legs gave way and I fainted.

○

When I opened my eyes, I was in my bed, Célestine holding one of my hands and Caroline the other

"You feeling better, Mama?"

I looked at my daughter's face creased with worry and beckoned her closer, she leaned over me and I took her in my arms and gave her a kiss

"Yes I'm feeling better"

but it wasn't true that I felt better, how could I be feeling better when my sister had just died? and what's more surely endured suffering that should never be inflicted on a human being, because we had long known what those bloodthirsty monsters supposedly heeding the call of a god who would not allow a single roumi to soil his lands were capable of doing to our Christian bodies for which they had no respect and never would

I rose unsteadily from the bed and Célestine and I set the table as we waited for Henri, who had gone to care for the ox and goats, Caroline and Gérald were in the garden tossing seeds to the hens

we ate our soup in silence, no one could think of a thing to say, not Célestine and not Henri either, who was watching me out of the corner of his eye afraid I

would faint a second time, the silence heavy as a winter
blanket, I wished someone would bring up the rain or
good weather but that surely was too much to ask, and
finally I said

"Where is my sister buried?"

everyone raised their heads as if I'd asked the one
question I wasn't supposed to ask

"We'll find out, Séraphine, but in this heat the soldiers usually bury bodies on the spot"

replied Henri as he placed his hand on my shoulder
to comfort me

"Well, I'd like to fetch her body and bury it beside
our two boys, that's my right, isn't it?"

"Yes, Séraphine, that's your right and that's what
we'll do, you can count on me"

I spent that first night with eyes wide open, swatting
at the mosquitos making my head spin, so enthralled by
the crickets' woeful songs and the endless whimpers of
bitches in heat that soon I lost control of my belly, my
arms and legs, every inch of my flesh

holy Mary mother of God

and grabbed Henri's hips in spite of myself, I pulled
his body onto mine so he would take me, break me, end
me, which is what he did, not truly understanding what
was happening

holy Mary mother of God

thrusting deep inside me until we both reached a
summit of pleasure that perhaps we hadn't reached in

a very long time, and after that I fell asleep, I was able to shut my eyes and forget this world, yes it was right after.

○

Early in the morning, in the cool of dawn, we took one of the village carts, accompanied by a few soldiers, and went to fetch my sister's body

I was seated beside Henri, who was holding the reins of a mule borrowed from Gaston Frick, the soldiers on foot in front and behind us, their wary eyes trained on every bush, tree, and rock behind which a fanatic might be lying in wait, even though the captain had sworn to us that there was nothing left to fear, that the army had done its job which was to bring peace to the region, having killed enough insurgents that no one in the nearby douars would think to pick up a weapon again

the sun was already high in the sky when we reached the plot Fernand had been working, at the top of the ridge where the house had been built there was nothing left but ash, the two wooden dovecotes had been burned to a crisp along with the barns, we could make out bits of charred beams mixed in with animal skulls, scraps of iron, tool smithereens, what looked like two or three plowshares, and in the two main rooms built of brick where my sister and Fernand must have lived, collapsed walls black with soot, a bed frame, a table, and four chairs missing their legs two wretches dressed in mended rags were aimlessly walking through what was left of the scorched fields of wheat and oats, upon seeing us they came closer, and just as quick the soldiers took aim

"Don't be frightened! we mean you no harm, my cousin and I did some work here now and then, m'sieur paid us to guard the cows"

I waved them over

"I'm Rosette's sister, did you know her?"

"Of course we knew m'sieur's wife! she was good to us and we were very saddened when we arrived in the morning and saw there was nothing left of the farm, nothing at all, everything burned to the ground, the animals too and I'd rather not say in what state we found m'sieur and m'dame, no, no, I'd rather not"

he turned his head to avert his gaze and blow his nose into his fingers

"Where are they buried?"

"There, under that tree"

he waved for us to follow

"The soldiers came with shovels and two coffins, because it wasn't possible to transport what was left of the bodies, what with the heat and all it wasn't possible, so they put the remains in the coffins and dug two holes in the ground"

the cousin stopped and pointed at the graves

"Right there"

and it was right there, the spot where my sister and her husband had been laid to rest beneath a cross

planted in the loose soil, and at the center of the horizontal plank nailed to a vertical plank someone had
etched the family name, *Gautier*, and nothing more, as
though the less that was said about what had happened
the better

I dug my nails into the palms of my hands for I felt
like screaming but it wasn't possible, not in front of
these men

forgive me, Rosette, for dragging you here, my poor
sister whose ambitions were humble, who was content
with little, my poor sister who I urged to cross the Mediterranean even though Louis had offered you his land
in Bourgogne and for whom a plot of vines would have
sufficed to make you happy for the rest of your life, but
Louis is dead, and now it's your turn beside your second
husband

my nails were digging so ferociously into my flesh
that I could no longer feel my hands

at last I said to the two men

"Would you help us dig up the coffins?"

"Of course, m'dame"

Henri distributed the shovels and pickaxes, it didn't
take us long to get the two plain wood coffins out of the
freshly turned earth, we put them in the cart, gave a few
coins to the poor wretches, and called back the soldiers
who'd gathered under a cork tree to smoke their pipes

the way back was even more somber than the way
there, it was stiflingly hot on that road with no shade,
the mule's head drooped as it pulled the cart whose

wheels resisted and squeaked with every spin, the solders were blowing off steam by chasing flies that couldn't be caught, and as Henri took big puffs from his pipe, squinting to soften the sun's glare burning his eyes, I steeped in my rage, silently sweating under my straw hat, not bothering to wipe away the drops soaking my forehead and dripping onto my cheeks and hands as if I was crying though I wasn't, as if I hadn't put every ounce of my strength into not crying

holy Mary mother of God, forgive me my pride and forgive me my rage

the soldiers left us at the village gate and Henri took the path that wound around the ramparts to the cemetery

some of our neighbors had already dug two holes beside my sons' graves, and the folks who knew us, with whom we were friendly, were there awaiting our return in the shade under the trees, and in the silence of that evening, which was greeted like every other evening by the disorderly flight of thousands of birds unabashedly enjoying the freedom of the sky, forever oblivious to the misery of man, everyone lent a hand, Gaston, Saturnin, Antonio, Adrien, Bobi, Jacquou, and little Albin, to carry the two coffins between the graves growing in number, spreading fast as twitch grass, soon enough the cemetery would have more dead in the ground than the village had living, César, Vincent, Jeannot, everyone pitched in to lower them with utmost care into the two holes

"In the name of the Father, the Son, and the Holy Spirit"

the priest said the customary words, shaking his aspergillum over the coffins, but I wasn't listening to him, not any more than I was the neighbors offering their condolences in hushed voices as they squeezed my hands, what could I have said back? my jaws were glued shut, my dry eyes locked in a dead stare, so I stood back and let the shovels drop earth onto the coffins with a noise I was beginning to know all too well and that my ears could no longer bear to hear

the noise of loose soil and pebbles hitting wood in the vengeful landslide to which our bodies are all fated sooner or later

so I stood back and let the others finish, after which they returned to the village with heads bowed and when only Henri and I remained, I decided it was time to kneel before the graves of our two boys and of Rosette and Fernand and Louis, the men, woman, and children who had been a part of our daily lives and whom we had loved and been loved by in return, yes, it was time to get on our knees and apologize for the harm we had brought upon them

and we got on our knees and we apologized

"Nicolas, François, and you, my darling sister, and Fernand and Louis"

I began, my mouth so dry the words caught in my throat

"Henri and I ask your forgiveness for dragging you into this risky venture, not you, Fernand, you got yourself into this mess, but my two boys, and you, Rosette, and your husband who had a dim view of our sea crossing, forgive me for not taking your opinions into account, Mama! Mama! you said, we don't want to go, and why not, boys? Because we're scared of the desert lions and the camels and the Arabs who are nothing like us! oh, my dear boys, forgive Henri and me for having been so stubborn, I know now that stubbornness gets you nowhere, it brings bad luck, and that when everything goes sour, it's best to go home, and that's what we're going to do, we're going home, because poor little Caroline can't bear much more, you should see her face, eyes so deep in their sockets that every morning I wonder if her body will hold on for even one more day"

"Are you sure you want to go back, Séraphine?"

said Henri

"Are you sure?"

but I wasn't listening, I wanted to finish my speech

"and you too, Henri, you can't bear any more either, your skin's turning yellow, all wrinkled from exhaustion, your chest is sunken, your eyes flush with fever every time a mosquito bites you, and as for me, must I repeat myself? I'm at the end of my rope, I can't even sleep anymore, can't eat when I'm supposed to eat or laugh when I'm supposed to laugh, if we don't go, Henri, if we don't leave as quickly as possible the malaria will get us in the end, and if it's not malaria, it'll be the cholera because that disease isn't done with us yet, and one day or another it'll come back to the village to finish the job it started"

I stared at the blazing horizon where the sun had disappeared, searching that beckoning vista for traces of all that threatened us

"Take a look at yourself, Henri, and take a look at me, don't you see what we're becoming? castaways, rags-and-bones, no, less than that, we're walking skeletons and this cursed Algerian land is eating us alive, God help us! it's eating our lungs and livers and guts, and our kidneys and hearts too, don't you see, Henri?! this land is ravenous and soon enough it will devour our souls"

searching and seething with rage as I calculated the possible escape routes to the sea.

○

Three months was all it took

the captain tried his best to change our minds but still we signed the document to relinquish our concession and we left

abandoning Célestine and her son, Gérald, our ox, our fields of wheat and oats, our garden where I'd managed to grow some tomatoes and a few patches of mint, abandoning the men and women who didn't want to admit defeat and who told us

"We'll get through this, stay!"

"No, we're going home to France"

"Stay, for heaven's sake!"

"No"

and standing before the graves of my two boys and my sister whom I got killed, I promised to return as soon as possible to bring their bodies back to France and give them the rest they deserved in a Christian cemetery

in our remaining days in the village we sold everything we could sell, it didn't bring in much but it was enough to buy tickets for the ship that we would be catching in Bône

we made sure to knock at every door and say goodbye to our poor settler friends who had been with us from the beginning, we kissed their hollowed cheeks and wept with them as they embraced us tightly, we paid a final visit to the captain, the army doctor, Sister Catherine, and the schoolmistress who by then had lost her rosy glow, and early the following morning we climbed into one of the carts in the convoy heading for Bône, Caroline, wrapped in a blanket, was still asleep, huddled against me, and I didn't have the courage to wake her so she could take a final look at the village and the cemetery where her brothers were buried

the day went by as all days of travel go by

and by late afternoon the three of us were aboard the *Sinai*, a steamer destined for Marseille, the gulf was

calm, not a cloud in the sky, we watched the Bône har-
bor recede in the distance as the city lit up, and then the
Sinai entered the black night

   plunged rather, prow, decks, and stacks, into the pu-
rifying darkness of the Mediterranean Sea

   as if that was our only passage out of hell.

○

must I say it?

   I never returned to Algeria to fetch the bodies of my
dearly beloved.

ACKNOWLEDGMENTS

The translator would like to thank Chris Clarke for his insight and feedback on this translation.

ABOUT THE AUTHOR

Mathieu Belezi is the author of more than a dozen novels. His writing career began with *Le petit roi*, which won the Marguerite Audoux Prize in 1999. His novel *Attacking Earth and Sun* has won the Prix Livre Inter and Le Monde Literary Prize. Having traveled widely and even taught in Louisiana, he now divides his time between France and Italy.

ABOUT THE TRANSLATOR

Lara Vergnaud is a translator of prose, creative nonfiction, and scholarly works from the French. She is the recipient of two PEN/Heim Translation Fund Grants and a French Voices Grand Prize, and has been nominated for the National Translation Award. She lives in France.